Someone's at the Door . . .

Cally watched her sister run up the walk to the front door.

She heard Kody grab the doorknob. Heard her start to push the heavy wooden door open.

Directing her gaze, Cally made the door stick.

Push as hard as you can, Kody, she urged silently. The door will not open.

It obeys my will.

I am the house and the house is me. I am part of the evil.

Put your shoulder into it, Cally urged. Go ahead—shove!

And now here's a greeting from your long-lost sister, Cally thought, summoning more evil energy.

Cally shot a dozen pointed steel spikes through the front door.

She listened gleefully as Kody's shrill screams rose up in a wail of terror.

Books by R. L. Stine

Fear Street

THE NEW GIRL
THE SURPRISE PARTY
THE OVERNIGHT
MISSING
THE WRONG NUMBER
THE SLEEPWALKER
HAUNTED
HALLOWEEN PARTY
THE STEPSISTER
SKI WEEKEND
THE FIRE GAME
LIGHTS OUT
THE SECRET BEDROOM
THE KNIFE
PROM QUEEN
FIRST DATE
THE BEST FRIEND
THE CHEATER
SUNBURN
THE NEW BOY
THE DARE
BAD DREAMS
DOUBLE DATE
THE THRILL CLUB
ONE EVIL SUMMER

Fear Street Super Chiller

PARTY SUMMER
SILENT NIGHT
GOODNIGHT KISS
BROKEN HEARTS
SILENT NIGHT 2
THE DEAD LIFEGUARD

The Fear Street Saga

THE BETRAYAL
THE SECRET
THE BURNING

Fear Street Cheerleaders

THE FIRST EVIL
THE SECOND EVIL
THE THIRD EVIL

99 Fear Street: The House of Evil

THE FIRST HORROR
THE SECOND HORROR
THE THIRD HORROR

Other Novels

HOW I BROKE UP WITH ERNIE
PHONE CALLS
CURTAINS
BROKEN DATE

Available from ARCHWAY Paperbacks

For orders other than by individual consumers, Archway Books grants a discount on the purchase of **10 or more** copies of single titles for special markets or premium use. For further details, please write to the Vice-President of Special Markets, Pocket Books, 1230 Avenue of the Americas, New York, NY 10020.

For information on how individual consumers can place orders, please write to Mail Order Department, Paramount Publishing, 200 Old Tappan Road, Old Tappan, NJ 07675.

99 FEAR STREET®: THE HOUSE OF EVIL

The Third Horror

A Parachute Press Book

AN ARCHWAY PAPERBACK
Published by POCKET BOOKS
New York London Toronto Sydney Tokyo Singapore

This book is a work of fiction. Names, characters, places and incidents are products of the author's imagination or are used fictitiously. Any resemblance to actual events or locales or persons, living or dead, is entirely coincidental.

AN ARCHWAY PAPERBACK *Original*

An Archway Paperback published by
POCKET BOOKS, a division of Simon & Schuster Inc.
1230 Avenue of the Americas, New York, NY 10020

ISBN: 0-671-88564-2

First Archway Paperback printing October 1994

10 9 8 7 6 5 4 3 2 1

Cover art by Bill Schmidt

Printed in the U.S.A.

IL 7+

The Third Horror

Chapter 1

Kody Frasier raised one hand to her forehead to shield her eyes from the sunlight. The house appeared unchanged from the street.

Several trees had been cut down and removed from the front yard, she saw. But the house and the lawn were still blanketed in heavy shade.

Stepping onto the gravel driveway, Kody felt a chill.

Two years, she thought. It's been two years since I said goodbye to this house.

Two years since I said goodbye to my sister Cally—to my little brother James.

Dead. Both of them.

Murdered by this dreadful house.

As Kody slowly made her way up the driveway, the

shade swept over her, cold as an ocean wave. Her legs suddenly became weak. She tugged on the sleeves of her pale green sweater, then jammed her hands into the pockets of her white denim jeans.

And stared up at the house that had brought so much horror and pain to her family.

Ninety-nine Fear Street.

The two-and-a-half-story house was nearly as wide as the yard. Its gray shingles were as stained and weather-beaten as Kody remembered them. The dark shutters were broken and peeling.

Kody hesitated on the driveway.

It's such a warm, sunny day, she thought. But the gloom of the house spreads over the front yard. The sunlight cannot break through.

Taking a deep breath, Kody forced herself to move forward.

The dark shingles on the porch roof were new, she saw. But the stained glass windows on either side of the front door were still faded and cracked.

She stared at the large number "99" on the warped wooden door.

Memories—frightening memories—made Kody stop again.

As she stared up at the house, the front door slowly swung open.

A girl stepped out from the darkness behind the door. She shook her blond hair and smiled at Kody.

Kody struggled to find her voice.

She opened her mouth wide and gasped in shock and horror.

The smiling girl stepped casually off the porch and waved.

"Cally—!" Kody called to her dead sister. "Cally—it's you!"

Chapter 2

The girl flashed Kody a taunting smile.

"Cally—!" Kody called again, her voice a choked whisper.

"Kody—are you okay?" the girl asked coldly.

Not Cally's voice, Kody realized. And the girl's dark eyes were not Cally's eyes.

All at once Kody recognized Persia Bryce, an actress who was Kody's age—eighteen.

"Persia, you s-surprised me," Kody stammered.

"Have you seen Bo?" Persia demanded, not the least bit interested in Kody's distress. Persia's eyes searched the front yard, where workers on the film crew were busily stretching cables and setting up equipment.

Still shaken, Kody stared at Persia's blond wig. The hair, Kody suddenly realized, was actually much shorter than Cally's had been. "No. I haven't seen Bo," Kody said softly.

"If you see him, tell him I'm looking for him," Persia instructed. She started jogging down the middle of the yard toward the row of trailers parked along the curb.

Kody watched Persia until she disappeared into one of the trailers. Persia had been the star of a TV sitcom called "Big Trubble." She had played Angela Trubble, the little girl in the sitcom family. But now Persia was grown and ready to try movies.

She always seems so nice during TV interviews, Kody thought with some bitterness. She's always so sweet and modest. Always acts like a girl who's surprised by her success.

Away from the cameras, Kody had discovered, Persia acted like a spoiled brat. She walked around with her nose in the air. Her expression said: *Stay away from me. I'm a star.*

Persia had two assistants who followed her around as if they were on short leashes. She was always calling out orders to them, and complaining when they didn't move fast enough.

Months before, when Kody had been introduced to the actress at the casting director's office in Los Angeles, Persia greeted her warmly. "It'll be fun working with you, actually playing *you* in this movie," Persia told her. "We'll be playing sisters, and I hope we can get to be like *real* sisters."

She's so nice, Kody had thought.

Then a few days later Kody learned that Persia had tried to have her removed from the movie. "I don't want to work with an amateur," Persia had complained.

Now, three months later, here they were in Shadyside. Ready to start filming the movie of Cally and Kody's lives—*99 Fear Street.*

And Persia wasn't even pretending to be friendly. She always stared at Kody with a look of disgust, as if Kody were some sort of insect. And when they weren't rehearsing, Persia didn't say a word to Kody. She talked only to the director, Bo Montgomery, or to her two assistants. She pretended that Kody didn't exist.

As Persia's trailer door slammed shut, Kody turned back to the house. Persia faded from her mind as Kody's thoughts returned to her dead sister.

Cally—are you in there? she wondered. Cally, I promised I'd come back for you. Will I find you in there? Will I?

I've got to make this picture work. This is my big chance, Bo Montgomery thought to himself. Gripping his clipboard in one hand, he stepped carefully over electrical cables in the attic, his eyes on the low ceiling. "Can we light this room—or should we build an attic back in the studio?" he asked the big man at his side, Sam McCarthy.

Bo stared at the associate producer's round, pink face and tiny blue eyes. McCarthy ran a hand over his stubby white hair. "We can light it, Bo," he replied.

"We've already started setting up the green goo in the floor. I think we can work with this space."

"Think?" Behind his blue sunglasses, Bo narrowed his eyes at McCarthy. *"Think* isn't good enough, Sam. You have to *know."*

Bo tugged at the sleeves of his gray sweatshirt. Then he put an arm around McCarthy's beefy shoulders. "You know what this picture means to me, Sam," he said with emotion. "After the last two turkeys I made, I thought I'd never get to direct another movie."

McCarthy snickered. "Hey, I helped you make those turkeys, chief. You don't have to remind me."

Bo's expression remained serious. "This film—*99 Fear Street*—is my last chance. I've *got* to make this movie work, Sam. I can't let anything go wrong."

McCarthy chewed on the unlit stub of a cigar he had wedged between his teeth. "What could go wrong?" he asked.

Bo frowned. "Plenty," he replied softly, staring around the narrow attic. "For one thing they're making me film in this run-down old house instead of on the studio lot in L.A."

"It's great publicity," McCarthy interrupted. "You're making the movie in the house where all the horrible stuff took place."

Bo scowled and shook his head. "The studio just doesn't want to spend any money, Sam. That's why they're making me film here. And that's why they stuck me with Kody Frasier playing Cally. I've got to use a total amateur in the starring role because they were too cheap to get me a real actress."

Bo sighed. "This role has Winona Ryder written all over it. Instead, I get Kody Frasier."

"But you said Kody tested well," McCarthy protested. "And she's had acting lessons, right?"

Bo didn't reply. Lowering his clipboard, he peered out the dusty attic window.

"You already got a spread in *People* magazine because of the sister," McCarthy continued. "It's great publicity, Bo. 'Kody Frasier Returns to the House of Horrors to Play Her Own Dead Sister.' Maybe she'll be terrific."

"She's *got* to be!" Bo replied heatedly. He tugged at his short ponytail. "Let's check out the basement."

As Bo led the way downstairs, a thousand thoughts bounced through his mind. Crew members he had to talk to, props to check, script problems to iron out, scheduling conflicts to be solved.

Directing a movie was never easy, Bo told himself. It was even harder when the pressure was on, when everything *had* to go smoothly—when a career depended on it.

As he and McCarthy explored the basement, Bo continued to think about all he had to do before shooting could begin. Lost in his thoughts, he didn't see the large gray rat scuttle out onto the concrete floor.

He didn't see the second rat, its long whiskers twitching excitedly, scamper silently out to join the first.

He didn't see the other rats creep out from the dark

walls and move to form a tight circle around the two of them.

The shrill chittering sound finally startled Bo from his thoughts. His eyes went wide behind the blue-lensed sunglasses. He grabbed McCarthy's arm and pointed.

"Sam—we're—surrounded!"

The rats' eyes glowed in the darkness. The chittering sound became a shrill hiss.

As if on a signal, the rats tightened their circle and rose on their hind legs.

The two men didn't have time to cry out—as the rats leaped to the attack.

Chapter 3

Uttering a startled cry, Bo swung the clipboard hard. It made a loud *thwack* as it connected with one rat. The stunned rodent went flying toward the wall.

Bo spun around, pulled a fat rat from the front of his sweatshirt. Kicked away another rat that had dived for his ankle.

Beside him, he could see McCarthy flailing his big arms, ducking low, slapping a screeching rat off his leg.

"Run! Move it!" Bo swiped at another hissing rat with the clipboard, catching it in the snout, sending it falling to the floor.

"Move!" he screamed over the shrill, excited rat cries. He shoved McCarthy hard toward the stairs.

They stumbled up the narrow steps, kicking rats off their sneakers, pulling them off their pants legs. Up to the hallway. Past several startled crew members. Out to the front yard.

Breathing hard, Bo stopped when he saw Kody Frasier in front of him on the walk. He could still hear the shrill hissing of the rats. He could still feel the prick of their claws on his skin.

"Bo—what's wrong?" Kody demanded.

"Uh—we have a bit of a rat problem," he said, trying to sound as casual as possible. No need to get the actors all excited. He called to one of the assistants. "Can you get an exterminator out here? Maybe two or three? Or ten?"

Kody shuddered, remembering the rats, their evil red eyes and how they had once attacked her. She pushed the thought aside. "Persia is looking for you," Kody told him.

Bo sighed. He raised his clipboard and glanced at the top page. "I'd better go see what she wants," he murmured. He gave Kody a quick wave and, forcing the leaping rats from his mind, jogged down to Persia's trailer.

"Kody—what's up?"

The voice made Kody turn. Rob Gentry, another actor, stepped toward her, his pale blue eyes trained on hers. Rob moved with an easy grace. Thin but athletic looking, he was at least a foot taller than Kody. "You okay?"

"Well . . ." Kody hesitated.

Rob slid a comforting arm around her shoulders. She had known him for only a week, but Rob was warm and outgoing. He acted as if everyone were an old friend. He was always flirting with Kody, putting an arm around her, teasing her as if he had known her forever.

"I'll get you a cup of coffee," Rob said, guiding her toward the caterer's trailer at the bottom of the driveway. "It must be really weird for you. Being back here, I mean. Making a movie about your own life."

He knows all about my life, about what happened to my family here, Kody realized. Everyone working here knows. They've all read the movie script.

The caterers had spread a long table with sandwiches, muffins, salads, fruits, and all kinds of cold and hot drinks. The food was available to everyone on the crew from morning till night. The caterers' table was a very important part of movie making, Kody had quickly discovered.

Rob poured a cup of coffee from a large silver pitcher and handed it to her. Kody added a lot of milk and two packets of sugar. She didn't really like the taste of coffee.

Rob poured himself a cup, then guided her away from the line of trailers to the next yard. He dropped onto the ground in front of a tall hedge and patted the grass, motioning for Kody to join him.

He has such a great smile, Kody thought. Rob's eyes caught the sunlight. His auburn hair was long and wavy, and brushed straight back.

He's the handsomest boy I've ever met, Kody found herself thinking as she lowered herself onto the grass beside him. "I didn't expect to feel so nervous," she told him. "I'm all jittery."

"I'm nervous too, you know," Rob confessed, sipping the steaming coffee slowly. "I mean, Anthony isn't exactly the biggest role. But this is my first film."

Rob had done some TV acting and a few commercials, Kody knew. His father was a Hollywood studio executive. "How else do you think I got this job?" he joked when Kody had first met him.

"Persia is being so awful," Kody said, sighing. "She orders me around as if I'm her dog."

"She's jealous," Rob replied, staring down into his cup.

"Huh? Persia? Jealous of me?" Kody cried in surprise.

Rob nodded. "She wanted your part. She wanted to play your sister Cally. She doesn't want to play you."

Kody let out a bitter laugh. "Who would want to play *me?*" she asked sarcastically.

Rob sipped his coffee thoughtfully. Then he raised his pale blue eyes to her. "You're not upset about Persia," he told her. "You're upset about being back here at your old house. Where it all happened."

"I—I thought I could handle it," Kody stammered, holding the cardboard cup between her knees. "I mean, seeing the house again. But as soon as I stepped onto the driveway, all the memories—all the horrible memories came flooding back."

"It must be tough," Rob murmured, shaking his head.

"I could feel them," Kody continued emotionally. "I could *feel* the memories. Pushing me back. Pushing me away from the house."

Rob raised his eyes to hers. Kody realized she was breathing hard. She took a deep breath, then let it out slowly.

"So why did you take the part?" Rob asked with genuine concern. "You knew it would be hard to face this place again—right?"

Kody nodded. "Two reasons," she replied thoughtfully. "One, it was such an incredible opportunity. I mean, my life was so terrible, Rob. My parents and I got as far away from Fear Street as we could. We moved to L.A. But our lives were—ruined."

She stifled a sob, took a deep breath, and continued. "My dad was blinded by something in this house. He never regained his sight. And my mother—she was never the same after James and Cally died. I tried to forget it all. I finished high school. I went to acting school. I guess I was desperate to be someone else. Anyone but me. And then I tried out for this movie—and they offered me the starring role. I—I had to do it."

A station wagon filled with kids rolled past slowly. They all gawked at the row of trailers, the workers, and the movie equipment in the front yard. "Are you a movie star?" a girl in the back called out to Kody.

Kody waved to the girl. The station wagon rumbled away.

"I had to do it," she repeated to Rob. "I have a second reason." Her hand trembled as she raised the cup to her lips and took a sip of coffee.

"What?" Rob asked, setting his cup on the grass, leaning back against the hedge.

"I made a promise to my sister that I'd come back," Kody revealed. She stared at the woods across the street. "I saw Cally in the window, the front window, on the day my mom and dad and I left. I saw Cally. Watching me from the window."

"Huh?" Rob sat up quickly, unable to hide his shock. "But your sister was dead!" he cried.

Kody nodded solemnly. "I know. But I saw her in the window. Seeing her there, pressed against the glass, so lost, and so sad—it's haunted me ever since."

He placed a hand on her shoulder. She saw him staring at her thoughtfully. She knew he didn't believe her story.

Who would believe it?

She continued anyway. "I promised Cally I'd come back. I promised her on that day two years ago that I'd come back, that I'd save her somehow." Kody sighed. "So here I am."

They were silent for a while. Then Rob climbed to his feet. He shook his head. "Weird," he muttered.

He started to say something else, but the assistant

director called to him. He turned and trotted off toward the house.

Kody took a last sip of coffee. She crumpled the cup in her hand and stood up.

Brushing off the back of her white jeans, she made her way to the driveway. I should get my script and go over the scene we're shooting tomorrow, Kody thought.

Thinking about the next day, the first day of shooting, made Kody's stomach feel fluttery. What if I can't do this? she wondered. What if the camera starts to roll and I freeze?

The rehearsals back in Los Angeles had gone pretty well. Bo Montgomery was a very understanding director. Very patient. Very soft spoken and kind.

But sitting around a table, reading lines from a script, was a lot different from standing in front of a movie camera and acting with two dozen crew members standing around watching, Kody told herself.

Kody could picture the gloating grin on Persia Bryce's face if she blew it.

Well, I'm not going to blow it, Kody assured herself.

She was so lost in her own troubled thoughts, she stumbled over a crate of special effects materials and nearly fell onto the driveway.

"Watch out—that box is filled with blood!" a crew member shouted.

"Sorry," Kody murmured, stepping around it.

Blood?

Yes. The movie will need lots of blood, Kody thought sadly.

She remembered the night more than two years before, when the blood started dripping from the ceiling in her parents' bedroom. The bright red blood, puddling on her parents' bed.

Her father—her poor father—had hurried up to the attic to see what was causing so much blood to drip. He had returned dazed and babbling, not making any sense at all, murmuring about three human heads, three bleeding human heads.

Poor Daddy, Kody thought.

If only we had run out of the house that night. If only we had run out and never looked back . . .

Halfway up the drive, Kody raised her eyes to the house—and gasped.

The living room window was curtained by shade. But even in the darkness Kody could clearly see the figure in the window.

She could see the girl's blond hair. See her sad expression. See her hands pressed against the glass.

"Cally!" Kody screamed.

Reaching out with both arms, Kody ran toward the front door. The gravel spun out from under her shoes as she ran.

She stopped at the front walk.

Is it Cally? Or is it Persia? she wondered, breathing hard.

Have I been fooled again?

Cally's ghost slid away from the window, floating back into the shadowy gloom of the house. The air pulsed around her. Sparks of dust rose up from the floor.

Her red eyes began to glow. Anger burst from her as a crackle of electricity. Workers in the next room cried out in surprise. A spotlight crashed.

"So my dear sister has returned!" Cally declared to herself, slipping back to the window for another look. The gray light filtering through the dusty glass poured through her. She could feel herself shimmering in and out of focus.

How long has it been, Kody? Cally's ghost wondered.

How many years has it been since you abandoned me here? Since you went off to live life? Since you left me to this cold shadow world?

I've lost all sense of time, Cally realized with a sob. There *is* no time for me.

I am *outside* of time.

But now Kody has returned.

Have you come searching for me, Kody? Cally wondered, unable to hold back her bitterness.

No. You haven't.

You've come back to be a movie star.

You've come back to play the role you always wanted to play, haven't you? You've come back to play *me!*

You were always jealous of me, Kody. So jealous you were *sick.*

And now you've gotten what you always wanted. You get to play me.

You're going to be a star—right, Kody? You're going to be rich and famous. All because *I* died.

All because you abandoned me to the evil of this house.

Cally continued to stare out into the gray front yard. The workers had taken a break. They were clustered around the food table at the foot of the driveway.

Cally watched only Kody.

She looks good, Cally thought. She let her hair grow. She lightened it so that it's *my* color now.

Kody sees me! Cally realized, glowing with sudden excitement. The air sparked and crackled around her.

Here she comes! Look at her—reaching out as if she wants to hug me. Look at her run. So eager—so eager.

Will you find me, Kody?

Yes, you will. Eventually.

But you'll see that I've changed, dear sister. I've changed a lot.

I am part of this house now. Part of the evil.

I am the evil and the evil is me.

You'll find that out, Kody, I promise you.

You won't be a movie star, Cally thought, shimmering in the rising dust. No, Kody, you won't be a movie star.

But you will be famous—as the actress who died while making a movie about *my* life!

Cally watched her sister run up the walk. Sliding through the shadows, the ghost moved to the front door.

She heard Kody grab the doorknob. Heard her start to push the heavy wooden door open.

Directing her gaze, Cally made the door stick.

Push as hard as you can, Kody, she urged silently. The door will not open.

It obeys my will.

I am the house and the house is me.

She heard Kody's surprised groan. Then she heard Kody give the door a hard shove.

Put your shoulder into it, Cally urged. Go ahead—shove!

And now here's a greeting from your long-lost sister, Cally thought, summoning more evil energy.

Cally shot a dozen pointed steel spikes through the front door.

She listened gleefully as Kody's shrill screams rose up in a wail of terror.

Chapter 4

Kody toppled backward as the steel spikes shot through the door. Before she could stop herself, she had let out a high-pitched cry.

The spikes had come so close.

I could have been *killed!* she realized.

She stared in horror at the sharp, pointed spikes sticking straight out from the door.

"What's happening here?" Bo Montgomery's voice broke through her terrified thoughts. "Kody—did you scream?"

She turned to face him, still trembling all over. "Bo! The door—" she managed to choke out, pointing.

Bo pulled off his blue sunglasses and stared at the rows of spikes in the door. His face reddened and twisted into an angry scowl. "Hey, McCarthy—!" he shouted. "McCarthy—get over here!"

He turned back to Kody. "I warned the special effects guys," he muttered. "Guess I'm going to have to chew McCarthy out."

Trying to force her breathing to return to normal, Kody studied Bo. He was a thin, intense, good-looking guy about thirty-five or forty, with a high square forehead and long, straight salt-and-pepper hair pulled back in a ponytail. He always had a day-old stubble of whiskers on his chin and cheeks.

He dressed the same every day—a gray sweatshirt, usually with a food stain or two on the chest, baggy, wrinkled chinos, and brown loafers without socks. He seldom removed his blue glasses, even at night.

He carried a clipboard with a stack of papers and charts and pages of the script, which he consulted constantly.

Kody had taken an instant liking to Bo. He had so much energy. He never stopped moving, and he never stopped talking. He did everything at a rapid pace. It was hard to keep up with him.

"McCarthy—let's move it, guy!" Bo called.

Sam McCarthy shouted something to two men at one of the trailers. Then he came lumbering across the front lawn toward Bo and Kody.

Kody had just met him that morning.

McCarthy removed the unlit cigar from his mouth as he stepped up to Bo. The end of the cigar, Kody saw, was wet and chewed-up. He wore gray work pants and a tight-fitting Grateful Dead T-shirt that didn't quite cover his bulging belly. McCarthy had beefy arms like those of a football player. His delicate hands didn't seem to belong to such arms.

"What's up, chief?" McCarthy asked Bo, breathless from hurrying up the lawn. He wiped sweat off his red forehead with the back of one hand. "You find a rat in your back pocket?"

Bo scowled. "No jokes, Sam." He pointed to the front door. "I warned you guys, we've got to know the plan here."

"Huh? What's the problem?" he asked.

"I need a list of what's in place and what isn't," Bo replied. "I know you've got green goo upstairs and blood ready too, right? But I'm not clear on what else is ready. And we nearly had a serious accident here, Sam."

Bo pointed to the front door. "Kody accidentally sprung the spikes. She could've been skewered like a roast on a spit."

McCarthy's eyes bulged, his round face turning even redder. "Hey, chief—we aren't doing spikes," he said, scratching his scalp through his short white hair.

"Where's the checklist?" Bo demanded.

"Ernie's got it," McCarthy replied. "He just went back to rigging the kitchen. But I know the list, Bo. And I know what we brought. No spikes. No way."

Kody shuddered. The house is up to its old tricks, she thought, edging closer to Bo.

"I want to see the list," Bo insisted stubbornly. "I should have a copy anyway." He turned to Kody. "You okay?"

Kody nodded. "I'm still a little shaky. But I'm okay—I guess."

McCarthy shoved the unlit cigar back into his mouth. He stared again at the steel spikes, frowning and muttering to himself.

Then his expression changed. "Hey, chief, got a second? I want to show you what Ernie and I rigged up in the kitchen. You're doing the garbage disposal scene first, right?"

Bo shuffled through the pages on the clipboard. "Yeah. First thing after break."

Kody swallowed hard.

Am I really going to relive that horrifying scene? she asked herself.

The memory rolled over her like an ocean wave. That night two years ago. She was in the house with Cally and Anthony, a boy Cally was going out with. The boy Rob was playing in the movie.

Anthony was helping out with the dishes after dinner. They heard his screams from the kitchen. They ran in to find him with his hand deep in the sink drain. The garbage disposal roaring.

Roaring . . .

Anthony's hand mangled and bloody.

Anthony screaming. Screaming over the roar of the disposal.

Later, when Anthony came out of the hospital, he wouldn't speak to Cally or Kody. And he never came near the house again.

And now here I am, Kody thought, back in the house. Ready to see the ghastly scene again.

Only this time it isn't real, she told herself.

This time, it's all pretend.

"Let's check it out," Bo said, lowering his clipboard. "Where's Rob? It's his scene." He spotted Rob in the driveway, talking to Angie, the script assistant. "Hey, Rob—time to work. Meet you in the kitchen," Bo shouted.

He turned back to Kody. "Where's Persia? She's in the scene too."

Kody shrugged. "I haven't seen her since—"

"Persia won't come out of her trailer," Rob reported, jogging across the grass.

"She—what?" Bo demanded.

"Persia says she won't come out until she gets her own fruit basket," Rob told the director. He winked at Kody. "The fruit on the table has all been pawed over and it's unsanitary."

Bo let out a moan and tossed his clipboard into the air. As he caught it, a strange smile crossed his face. "Know what I should do? I should tell Persia's parents how their little girl is behaving."

"That won't help," Rob replied.

"Why not?" Bo demanded.

"Persia's parents *work* for her," Rob told him. "Her mom is her secretary. Her dad is her manager."

Bo's smile faded. "All right. Come on, guys. Let Persia sit in her trailer. We'll check the kitchen out without her."

Bo pushed open the front door. Kody followed him into the house, a hundred horrifying memories shoving into her mind at once.

The pounding of hammers and the shrill whine of a power saw cut through Kody's thoughts. The crew had spread out over the living room, setting up lights, painting, wallpapering, moving furniture into place—the finishing touches.

From the front entryway, Kody trained her eyes on the living room window. *If Persia is still in her trailer, who did I see in the window?* Kody asked herself.

She didn't have time to think about it. Rob pulled her back into the kitchen.

Kody took a deep breath and held it. She expected to be overwhelmed by the kitchen, by the memories it would bring back.

But the room had been completely rebuilt—new cabinets, new appliances, new floor, new everything. Kody was relieved that she didn't receive the emotional jolt she expected.

After stepping over a bundle of electrical cables, they made their way to the sink. McCarthy's tiny blue eyes lit up as he motioned to the drain. "I think this will work out really well," he said. He grabbed Rob's arm. "Here. Stick your hand in."

"Huh?" Rob pulled back.

"It won't bite you," McCarthy insisted, grinning around the stub of his wet cigar. "Put your hand in the drain. All the way in. Then pull it out."

Rob hesitated. Bo motioned impatiently with the clipboard. "Give him a demo, Sam. Run through it for him."

McCarthy shrugged. "It's simple. You just stick

your hand all the way in the drain. Then you start to scream your head off."

"You mean over the sound of the garbage disposal?" Rob asked, peering warily into the drain.

Bo shook his head. "No garbage disposal sound," he told Rob. "We'll put the grinding sound in later at the studio."

"Yeah. Now, when you stick your hand in," McCarthy continued, "you'll slip it into a special rubber glove. The glove is positioned in the drain. You slip your hand all the way in. Then you pull it out. The glove has blood all over it and the fingers are all chewed up. It looks great."

"Gross," Rob muttered.

Kody lingered behind them, trying to force away the horrifying memories. This is a movie, she repeated to herself. This is a movie.

"We'll need the water running, right?" Bo asked, rubbing his chin.

"Yeah. Here," McCarthy replied. He reached out and turned the knob. Cold water streamed from the sink faucet into the drain.

"The glove is positioned so it won't fill with water," he explained to Rob. "Go ahead. Give it a try." He motioned to the drain.

"We'd better try it two or three times," Bo suggested. "I want to make sure the rubber glove stays in place."

Rob stepped up to the sink and stuck out his hand, peering down into the drain.

Kody stepped closer to get a better view.

Water splashed into the sink.

Rob lowered his hand to the drain. Again he hesitated. Then he raised his hand and shook his head, frowning.

He turned to Bo. "I'm sorry. I just have the weirdest feeling."

"We need to rehearse this," Bo insisted calmly. "Go ahead. Just take the plunge, man."

"You need to get the feel of the rubber glove," McCarthy added. "Go ahead. There's nothing down there that can hurt you."

Rob glanced at Kody, his cheeks pink. She could see that he was embarrassed to be making such a big deal about this.

She moved up beside him.

He leaned over the sink. Then he lowered his hand toward the drain.

Lower. Lower.

"Here goes," he said softly.

Chapter 5

Kody stared into the sink.

Water from the faucet splashed onto Rob's hand. The bright overhead lights reflected in the aluminum sink made the water shimmer and gleam.

Rob hesitated once again. He stood up. "I—I'm sorry," he stammered, shaking his head. His auburn hair fell over his forehead. "I'm just having trouble—"

"Step back, son," McCarthy said gently. He put a hand on Rob's shoulder and guided him back. Kody followed. "You know what your problem is? You've read the script! You know what happens!"

Everyone laughed. Tense laughter.

"I try to get my actors not to read ahead. But they just won't learn," Bo joked.

"Is that why you won't give us the last ten pages of the script?" Kody asked.

Bo grinned at her. "No one knows the ending except me," he told her. "I want everyone to be surprised."

McCarthy stepped up to the sink and turned to Rob. "Now, watch. I'll run through it once. Then you try—okay?"

"Thanks," Rob replied, blushing. "I'm sorry I'm acting like such a jerk."

"We'll all act like jerks before this picture is over," Bo assured him. "Everyone except *me,* of course."

More tense laughter.

Kody and Rob stepped up to watch.

McCarthy leaned over the sink. "Do it in one quick motion, like this," he told Rob.

McCarthy plunged his hand into the drain.

Kody let out a startled cry as she felt someone push her hard from behind and she bumped the sink front.

Her cry was instantly drowned out by the grinding of the garbage disposal as it churned to life.

The grinding became a roar.

McCarthy's mouth dropped open. The cigar stub fell into the swirling water in the sink.

The swirling *red* water.

An almost inhuman screech burst from deep inside McCarthy.

As he pulled back, falling away from the sink, his arm shot up in the air.

The rubber glove dropped to the floor with a wet *smack.*

McCarthy gripped his wrist, holding the hand high above him, staring up at it, howling, howling like a wild animal.

Kody swallowed hard and stared at the hand.

Blood spurted up into the air, flowed down McCarthy's arm.

Red as raw hamburger, McCarthy's fingers fell loosely on his cut and mangled palm.

No! Kody thought. No—this isn't happening! This isn't happening again!

Then McCarthy's howling drowned out all other thoughts.

Chapter 6

"I'll make this short," Bo said, tilting his chair back and crossing his legs. He rubbed his stubble of a beard with one hand. His eyes, usually lively and intense, appeared red rimmed, tired. He replaced his blue glasses. "It's been a long day—for everyone," he said softly.

He had called them into the trailer he used as an office. Sitting between Rob and Persia, Kody glanced out the trailer window at the setting sun, red behind the dark silhouettes of trees.

Rob leaned forward in his folding chair. He hadn't changed. His shirt had dark splashes of blood on the front.

Persia yawned loudly. She twirled her blond wig in

her hands. Her own crimped black hair hung down to her shoulders.

"When Bud and I did our research for the script," Bo continued, "we ran across a lot of strange stories about this street. Fear Street. Of course, we didn't really believe any of them. . . ."

"They're true," Kody murmured. "I—lived one of them."

Rob squeezed her hand. She saw Persia roll her eyes obnoxiously.

"Well, I'm not sure if I'm ready to believe them yet or not," Bo said, frowning. "But after what happened to McCarthy a few hours ago, I think we all have to be super careful."

"Is he going to be okay?" Rob asked.

Bo shrugged. "I got word from Shadyside General. He's resting comfortably. But they can't fix his hand. He's going to lose all the fingers." He removed his glasses again and pinched the bridge of his nose.

Rob let out a gasp. Kody swallowed hard. "How awful," Persia murmured.

Glancing up, Kody realized that Bo's eyes were locked on her.

"Did you stumble, or what?" Bo asked.

"Huh?" Kody didn't understand.

"In the kitchen," he said softly. "You fell forward and bumped the garbage disposal on. I saw you."

"No—!" Kody started to protest. "It wasn't me. I mean . . ." Her voice trailed off. "I don't know what happened. . . ."

"I know how freaked you must be," Bo said. "To be

back here, in the house and all. But we're behind you, Kody. We're pulling for you. We all know you're going to be terrific." He flashed Persia a meaningful look.

Persia continued twirling the wig and pretended she wasn't interested.

"I hope you can keep it together," Bo told Kody. "I mean, you're terribly important to this production."

He's blaming me for McCarthy's accident, Kody realized. He doesn't want to come right out and say it. He doesn't want to say, "You pushed the button that started up the disposal and ruined McCarthy's life." So he's giving me a pep talk instead.

"I'm going to do my best," Kody vowed in a low voice. "I really want to do well, Bo. I know you went out on a limb for me."

"All for the publicity," Persia muttered, her eyes on Rob.

Bo leaned forward in his chair, narrowing his eyes at Persia. "What did you say?"

Persia continued to fiddle with the blond wig. "I said you hired Kody for the publicity. You know. So all the magazines will write about how the actual sister is playing a part in her own family's horror movie."

Bo's mouth dropped open. His cheeks colored behind the stubble. "I hired Kody because she's a talented actress," he told Persia. He said it softly, patiently, as if explaining something to a child.

"I really hate this wig. It's so tacky," Persia complained.

She was deliberately changing the subject, Kody realized. Persia had gotten her nasty dig in about why Kody was hired. That's all she cared about.

"Talk to Wardrobe," Bo told her.

Persia held the wig up in front of her. "I guess it's supposed to be tacky." She turned to Kody. "It's supposed to look like *you*—right?"

Kody opened her mouth to utter an angry reply.

But Rob broke the tension by laughing. He put a hand on Persia's shoulder. "Hey, Persia—don't be so friendly. You'll ruin your image."

Persia made a disgusted face and wriggled her shoulder out of Rob's grasp. "Rob, you were *great* in your dog food commercial," she said nastily. "Really. That was your *best* work!"

"Come on, guys—!" Bo pleaded. "We start shooting tomorrow. We've got to work together—right? And by the way, we won't be doing the kitchen scene. It's going to take a while to clean up in there. We're going to do some close-up stuff instead. You know. Reaction shots. In the backyard. Just to get warmed up."

Rob let out a sigh of relief.

The light in the trailer suddenly faded. It took Kody a few seconds to realize that something had blocked the sunlight from the window. She turned to see a face staring in at her.

"Ohh." Kody let out a low cry as she recognized the man.

He was so pale. His round black eyes peered in at her.

What was his name? Where did she know him from?

"Who *is* that?" she cried.

"Oh. Yeah. I've got to go talk to him," Bo said, getting up from the chair. He had to stoop. "His name is Lurie, I think. He's a local real estate guy. He's leasing us the house. See you later, guys. Get lots of sleep, okay? I want beautiful faces tomorrow."

He pushed past them and lowered himself out of the trailer.

Lurie. Lurie.

He looks so familiar, Kody thought, a knot of dread tightening in her stomach.

Was he the man who sold Daddy the house two years ago?

She struggled to remember as she followed Rob and Persia out onto the street.

At the bottom of the driveway the catering crew was packing up. Electrical workers on the front lawn were closing up their cases, putting away equipment, preparing to leave.

"There's the car to take us to the hotel," Rob said, pointing. "You coming?"

"I have my own car," Persia told him. "Besides, I've rented a house. I'm not staying in a hotel."

"I'm coming," Kody said.

But Persia blocked her path. "Listen, Kody, I—I—

want to apologize for my jokes," she said, her dark eyes studying Kody. "I have a rotten sense of humor. Everyone tells me that." She shrugged.

"That's okay," Kody replied, trying not to show how surprised she was by this unexpected apology.

"Well, I just wanted to tell you one thing, Kody," Persia continued, speaking in a low, confidential voice. "If you're too freaked out by all this—I mean, if you're too scared and upset, I think everyone will understand if you drop out of the picture." A cruel smile formed on her full lips.

"You mean *quit?"* Kody cried angrily.

Persia nodded, her smile growing wider.

"No way!" Kody insisted shrilly. "No way, Persia! I'm going to act in this movie whether you like it or not!"

"Don't raise your voice to me," Persia snapped haughtily. "I was just trying to save you from embarrassing yourself."

"Well, I don't need your help!" Kody sputtered, balling her hands into tight fists.

"You need all the help you can get!" Persia uttered.

Kody wasn't really sure what came next or how the fight started. It all happened so fast.

Did she shove Persia?

Did Persia shove her?

Were they really grappling with each other, wrestling, trying to knock each other down?

It all seemed to be outside them, part of a movie, a really violent action movie. Except that it *hurt* when

Persia pulled Kody's hair. And Kody's heart was pounding so hard, she had to struggle to breathe.

And then Persia's fist struck hard. So hard.

"Persia—stop!"

Was that Kody shrieking like that?

"Stop! You're *hurting* me!"

Chapter 7

Strong hands grabbed Kody by the shoulders and pulled her back. "Whoa!" Bo called. "Whoa! Easy now! Whoa!"

Rob stepped in front of Persia, blocking her from Kody.

Bo pulled Kody into the shade of the trailer. Her chest heaving, gasping for breath, she pressed her back against the metal wall.

Bo moved toward Persia, bewildered. "What was *that* about?" he demanded softly.

Bo always stays calm, Kody realized, trying to slow her racing heart. The angrier he gets, the quieter he speaks.

"Just getting in the mood," Persia replied, pushing

damp strands of crimped black hair off her forehead. "I mean, I'm trying to get the feelings right."

"Huh?" Rob gaped at her in disbelief. "You mean—?"

Bo shook his head, frowning at Persia.

"Kody and I are very competitive sisters, right?" Persia said, straightening the bottom of her tank top. "We don't get along. So I'm just trying to get into character. I'm just trying to get my angry juices flowing. You know. Get into the competitive spirit."

"But, Persia—" Kody protested.

Persia opened her eyes wide as she turned to Kody. "Hey, you didn't think I was really angry—did you? You knew I was acting, right?"

Persia didn't give Kody a chance to reply. "If you couldn't tell I was acting, you really *are* in bad shape!" she declared.

Persia is doing everything she can to make me look bad in front of Bo, Kody realized.

Bo rubbed his chin, his eyes on Persia. "I appreciate your dedication," he said dryly. "But it's a little late for rehearsing, don't you think?"

"Whatever," Persia muttered. *"Ciao,* everyone." She waved, flashing Kody a triumphant smile. Then she turned and made her way quickly to the white stretch limo waiting for her at the end of the line of trailers.

"I don't *believe* her!" Kody declared, starting to feel a little more normal.

"Save your anger," Bo told her. "Remember how

you feel right now. Save it for when we shoot. You'll need it." Shaking his head, he hurried up the lawn to talk to the sound crew.

"You okay?" Rob asked, his expression concerned.

"Yeah. I guess," Kody replied shakily. "Persia really thinks she can get away with anything—doesn't she!"

"She probably can," Rob replied seriously. "Ready to go to your hotel?" He pointed to the black car waiting across the street.

"Know what? I'm going to cool out in my trailer for a while," Kody replied. "Just till I catch my breath. Send the car back for me—okay?"

She could see disappointment on Rob's face.

I think he likes me, Kody thought. The idea pleased her.

But then she told herself: Rob seems to like *everyone.* He's a really friendly, warm, outgoing guy.

Don't start getting ideas, Kody, she scolded herself. Rob grew up in Beverly Hills. He's been around movie and TV stars his whole life.

Why would he be interested in me?

But then, to her complete surprise, he leaned forward, wrapped his arms around her shoulders, and kissed her.

A long kiss. A hungry kiss.

Kody felt so startled, she just stood there at first. But then she eagerly returned the kiss, moving her mouth over his.

He turned away quickly, ending the kiss, and

started toward the car with long, loping strides. "I'll be in my room later," he called back to her. "If you want to call me."

She watched him climb into the backseat of the car. He gave her a quick wave as the driver pulled away.

Kody shut her eyes. She could still taste Rob's lips on hers.

Does he really like me? she wondered.

Or was he just acting? Like Persia. Trying to get into character.

He's just an actor. They're all actors.

She realized she wasn't thinking clearly. It had been such an upsetting, exciting, horrifying day—a day of one emotion piling on top of another.

She climbed the three low steps and pushed open the door to her trailer. The sun had lowered behind the trees. She stepped into the darkness, pulled the door shut behind her, and made her way blindly to the low couch against the wall.

Darkness. Cool, quiet darkness, she thought.

She lay down and stretched out on the unfamiliar couch. The leather felt cool against her skin. The air inside the trailer smelled stale. She lowered an arm over her eyes, seeking complete darkness.

I probably should have gone back to the hotel, she thought. But I need a few minutes alone. A few minutes to catch my breath. To think.

She pictured Persia. Persia's taunting eyes. Persia's cruel smile.

How am I going to deal with her? How? Kody wondered.

I can't ignore her. We'll be working together for weeks and weeks. We have so many scenes together.

I can't try to compete with her. There's no way I can be as sarcastic and cutting. And I don't want to be.

I can't compete with her. But can I get along with her?

With these troubled thoughts floating through her mind, Kody drifted into a troubled sleep.

A knock on the door startled her awake.

At first, staring into blackness, she had no idea where she was. The coolness of the leather couch under her hands reminded her.

When did I fall asleep? she wondered. How long have I been sleeping?

Her T-shirt clung to her back. Her throat felt dry and sore.

She reached out, struggling to find the lamp switch. But she lowered her hand when she heard the knocks.

Three short, soft knocks.

Tap tap tap.

A pause. Then three more.

Tap tap tap.

"No!" she cried in a choked whisper.

The soft tapping on the trailer door sent chills down her back.

She jumped to her feet.

I remember those knocks.

Yes, I remember them. The soft knocks of a ghost.

Standing stiffly in the darkness of the narrow trailer, Kody froze.

Tap tap tap.

The same sounds Kody had tapped on Cally's bedroom door.

Two years ago. Kody had pretended to be a ghost. Late at night she had knocked softly like that on her sister's door.

Three soft taps, then three more.

But now Cally was dead. And Kody was standing frozen in a strange, dark trailer, her neck tingling with fear, her skin cold, her heart thudding, listening—listening to the same soft taps.

Remembering.

Listening.

"Cally—is that you?"

Tap tap tap.

Kody dove for the door. Pushed it open with both hands.

And peered out.

Chapter 8

No one there.

Kody stared out at the front yard of her old house.

No one. The workers had all left.

"Cally—were you here?" Kody whispered. "Did you knock on my door?"

Silence.

Somewhere down the block a baby was crying.

Kody saw a yellow beam of light darting near the house. The light from a flashlight carried by one of the night security guards. The beam played over the shrubs against the front wall, then disappeared around the side of the house.

Without realizing it, Kody stepped out and wandered onto the grass. She stared up at the house, looming black against the purple evening sky.

The two upstairs windows seemed to stare down at her like eyes—cold, unfeeling eyes. That was my bedroom, she remembered. And Cally's was down the hall.

Kody swallowed hard. She missed her sister so much.

She moved closer, drawn to the house.

Drawn back to her memories.

Wet grass clung to her sneakers. A heavy dew had fallen.

Somewhere down the block the baby continued to cry. Short, shrill howls.

Kody stepped over cables and around metal cases of equipment and made her way to the window beside the front door.

Here I am, standing on this spot again.

Staring into this house. Into this dark living room.

A dim light in back.

She blinked. Once. Twice.

Is it just my imagination? My eyes playing tricks on me?

No. Pale light filtered into the hallway, casting long shadows over the carpet.

Someone left the kitchen light on, Kody realized. Maybe they're still working in there. Maybe they're still cleaning up.

Once again she pictured Sam McCarthy holding his hand up. The blood spurting over his arm. The lifeless, mangled fingers.

Are they working in the kitchen?

Or, Cally, is it you?

Cally. Cally. Cally.

Cally, you're the real reason I came back, Kody thought, moving to the front door.

Pushing the door open. Stepping into the narrow entryway.

Cally, I promised I'd come back to find you. I saw you the day we left, watching so sadly from the window. I saw you, Cally.

And now I've come back to keep my promise.

Are you here, Cally? Is that your light in the kitchen?

Have you been in this house these past two years, waiting, waiting for me?

Crazy thoughts, Kody knew. Such crazy, frightening thoughts.

But here she was. Walking silently through the back hallway. Toward the light. The pale light from the kitchen.

And now, here she was in the kitchen doorway.

Staring at the figure bent over the sink.

Staring at her in shock.

Covering her mouth to keep from crying out.

Chapter 9

Kody sank back into the shadows. She didn't want to be seen.

Is that really Mrs. Nordstrom? she asked herself.

Is that really our old housekeeper scrubbing the sink?

Staying close to the wall, Kody leaned warily into the kitchen. The old woman had her back to Kody as she bent over the sink, scrubbing vigorously. But Kody recognized her.

What is she doing in this house after everyone has left? Does she still come here every day? Does she still work here?

"Mrs. Nordstrom!" Kody called out, hurrying across the kitchen.

The old housekeeper turned from the sink, her mouth open in surprise. She squinted across the room. "Cally—is that you?"

Kody stopped in the center of the room. "No, it's Kody. I'm Kody."

Mrs. Nordstrom wiped her hands on a dish towel. Her hands still dripping, she moved forward and wrapped Kody in a quick, wet hug. "What a surprise, child. It's been so long! How is your family?"

"Okay," Kody replied. "I mean, better. They're living in Los Angeles. They—well—you know, Mrs. Nordstrom."

The old woman *tsk-tsk*ed. "So much sadness," she murmured. "The family that moved in after you. So much sadness for them too. The boy was about your age. Brandt. He died too." She shook her head. "So sad."

Kody shuddered. "You look exactly the same, Mrs. Nordstrom. I guess I'd better let you get back to work."

"I'm scrubbing the blood," Mrs. Nordstrom replied sadly. "It's so hard to scrub up." She turned back to the sink. "Come see me again—okay, child?"

"Okay," Kody replied softly. She backed away, watching the housekeeper, who hummed to herself as she scrubbed at the dark bloodstains in the sink.

Kody backed into the comforting darkness of the hallway. Then turned into the living room. Stepping over the electrical cables, she waited for her eyes to adjust.

The furniture was all strange. All new. The set designers had brought all the furniture from Los Angeles.

Kody made her way into the room, running her hand over the low crushed-velvet couch, stepping around an ottoman.

"Cally—are you here?" The whispered words slipped from her mouth as her eyes scanned the dark room. "Cally? It's me. I've come back for you."

She stood stiffly in the center of the room and waited.

For what?

A whispered reply? A laugh? A cold gust of wind that would tell her that her sister was there with her?

"Cally? I know you can hear me," Kody said, raising her voice, keeping it low and steady. "I know you're still in this house, Cally."

And then she *did* feel her.

Kody gasped as the feeling swept over her. Just a chill at first. A cold shudder.

A heavy presence in the room.

"You *are* here! I can tell!" she whispered excitedly, feeling her heart pound.

The presence came closer. The feeling grew stronger.

"I can *feel* you, Cally!" Kody cried. "I *know* you're here with me. I—I just know!"

The blood pulsed at Kody's temples. The whistling in her ears grew louder as she strained to listen, to hear a signal, a whisper, a sigh, that would reveal Cally's presence.

"Cally—you're here. I know you're here."

Before she could turn around, the ghostly hand of her sister slipped over Kody's shoulder and began to tighten around it.

Chapter 10

"Cally?"

Kody turned as the hand loosened its grip.

And stared into a blinding light.

It was not her dead sister who had grabbed her.

"What are you doing in here, miss? How did you get in?" The security guard, a stern-looking middle-aged man with a face pushed in like a bulldog's frowned at her suspiciously. He shone his flashlight at her, a harsh spotlight.

"I—I— The door was open," Kody stammered. She raised both hands to shield her eyes from the bright light.

"But why are you here?" the guard demanded impatiently.

"I just came in," Kody blurted out. "I mean, I used to live here, and—I'm in the movie—and—"

"You're the sister!" the guard exclaimed excitedly. He lowered the light. "You're the sister, right? I read all about you. A long article. In *People* magazine."

"Yeah. I'm the sister," Kody replied weakly. She had been so certain that Cally was near. She had felt the energy. So much energy in the air, in the room—everywhere.

But now it was gone. Kody suddenly was drained. Weary.

"Everyone's left, miss," the guard told her. "There's just the cleaning woman here."

"I should go too," Kody said, turning toward the doorway. "Sorry if I frightened you."

"That's okay," the guard said, rubbing his pug nose with the end of the flashlight. "At least you weren't a burglar. Or a looter. If you were, I'd have had to shoot you!" He let out a strange, almost silent laugh.

"Well, good night," Kody said, eager to get away.

She was nearly to the front door when the guard called for her to stop. "Just one more thing, miss," he said, hurrying across the room to her.

"Yes?"

"Could I have your autograph?" he asked shyly. And then he added, "It's for my nephew."

"I want to try the zoom close-up first," Kody heard Bo telling the assistant director. Kody hurried across the back lawn, feeling nervous and excited and eager to get started.

She had spent nearly an hour with the makeup girl. Her hair felt heavy from all the hair spray. And the powdery makeup was already making her face itch.

Waving to Rob, who stood beside Bo, Kody made her way through the dozens of crew members. They were scurrying around, making sure everything was ready for the morning's shoot.

It was a little before seven. An orange sun was still low in the brightening sky. The early morning air carried a chill.

"I'm ready!" Kody called breathlessly to Bo.

He didn't hear her. He was busy talking to Ken, the technical director, gesturing with his clipboard, clapping Ken on the back with his free hand.

"Are you nervous?" Rob asked, stepping up close to Kody, so close she could smell his aftershave. He wore a white polo shirt and straight-legged black denim jeans.

"You're wearing more makeup than me!" Kody blurted out.

Rob laughed. "That's showbiz!"

"I hate it that you're better looking than me!" Kody exclaimed.

She immediately regretted saying that. Rob seemed genuinely embarrassed.

She forced a laugh. "Sorry. I guess I *am* a little nervous. I don't know *what* I'm saying."

He squeezed her hand gently. His hand was warm, hers cold and wet. "You'll do fine. We're just doing reaction shots," he told her. "You don't have to say a single line today."

"Stand back. I want to test the boom camera." Bo gently ushered Kody and Rob out of the way. "Hey, you look great, Kody. Feel okay?"

He hurried back to tell Ken something before Kody could answer.

Kody turned back to Rob. "Why is the camera up so high?"

"Bo wants to do some zoom-in horror shots," Rob explained, brushing a fly off his shirt. "You know. They do them in every horror movie. You scream your head off, and the camera comes zooming down on your face."

"So the camera comes sliding down that pole?" Kody asked, staring up at it.

"Yeah. The pole is called a boom," Rob told her.

She grinned at him. "You know everything, huh?" she teased.

"I know enough," he replied, smiling back at her.

She thought he might lean over and kiss her right there, right in front of everyone.

But Bo interrupted, bursting between them. "Where's Persia?" he demanded of no one in particular. He scribbled on his notepad. "Have you seen Persia? She's up first."

"I saw her limo arrive," Rob said.

"So where is she?" Bo asked, searching the backyard.

"Still in Makeup," a crew member yelled.

"Is there a stand-in?" Bo demanded impatiently. "I want to test the camera."

Kody saw a girl in a sleeveless blue T-shirt and

bright blue Lycra bicycle shorts step forward. She was the same size as Persia, with short brown hair and a tense, no-nonsense expression.

"Are you doing lighting? Should I put on my wig?" she asked Bo.

"No. Just positioning," Bo told her. "What's your name, hon?"

"Joanna," she replied, moving up beside Bo.

"Aren't you cold in that outfit?" he asked.

Joanna nodded. "I thought it would be warmer. But there's not much sun back here. It's so dark."

Bo put his hands on her shoulders and guided her into position under the boom. "Don't move. That's perfect. Turn to the camera."

"Do you want me to scream or anything?" Joanna asked.

Bo had turned to say something to the camera operator, a lanky young man with long straight black hair and a black mustache.

Joanna crossed her arms over her chest and waited.

"No. Just stand," Bo told her, his eyes on the papers on his clipboard. "We'll let Persia do the screaming—if she ever gets out of Makeup."

Rob leaned close to Kody and whispered, "I can't believe Persia is late the first day."

"I believe it," Kody replied dryly.

They took a few steps back as crew members prepared for the camera test. Kody glanced quickly around the backyard. There were at least twenty crew members scurrying around, talking, moving cables, checking equipment, or waiting for Bo's next instructions.

"Okay, let's try one," Bo called loudly.

The crew instantly became silent.

Bo put a hand on Joanna's shoulder and gestured up to the camera with his clipboard. "It's going to come sliding down the boom toward you," he told her. "Slowly at first, then picking up speed. It'll stop right here." He held his hand a foot from Joanna's face.

"Should I face it like this?" she asked, staring up at the heavy black camera perched so high above the ground.

"Yeah. Good," Bo said, patting her shoulder. "You can try a scream if you like. Might be good practice."

Bo checked his watch. "Ready, Ernie?"

Rob had his arm around Kody's shoulders. They both moved closer to get a better view.

Ernie, the boom operator, flashed Bo a thumbs-up sign.

"Let it slide on three," Bo instructed. He nodded at Joanna. Then he counted slowly, "One—two—three."

Kody saw Ernie release a lever.

Joanna raised both hands in the air and let out a shrill scream as the big camera started its slide.

It slipped down slowly at first, then moved faster. Faster.

Joanna's scream stopped abruptly as the camera smashed into her face with a sickening crack.

Her arms shot straight out.

Like everyone else, Kody stared in silent disbelief.

For a few seconds Joanna seemed suspended there, her head impaled by the protruding lens.

Then she toppled back and fell heavily to the ground, leaving the camera soaked with her bright red blood.

Chapter 11

Kody buried her face in Rob's shoulder. "Is she—? Rob, is Joanna—?"

Rob didn't reply.

Shrill, panicky cries rang out over the yard.

"Call an ambulance!"

"Don't move her!"

"Is she conscious?"

"Where's the phone? Who's calling for help?"

"Try to stop the bleeding!"

"Her eyes! Did it smash her eyes?"

Kody pictured the camera sliding again, sliding down so hard into Joanna's face. And again Kody heard the sickening sound of the collision. The *crack* that had to be the splitting of Joanna's skull.

"Let's go to my trailer," Rob suggested quietly, his arms around Kody. "We can't be of any use here."

As he guided her toward the house, Kody heard Ernie, the camera operator, shouting to Bo. "The bolts on the catch were all loosened," Ernie called, his voice choked with alarm. "Bo—the catch was totally loose!"

Kody stopped to watch.

Bo hurried toward the camera boom. But a man in a gray uniform stepped forward to block his way.

The security guard! Kody recognized the security guard from the night before. He was talking rapidly to Bo—and pointing at Kody.

Bo turned and his eyes narrowed as they locked on Kody. "Could you come here for a second?" he called.

A crowd had huddled around the fallen stand-in. Over the excited, horrified voices of the crew, Kody could hear the wail of sirens growing louder. The ambulance was on its way.

"Should I wait for you?" Rob asked.

Kody shook her head. She hurried over to Bo.

"Kody, were you here last night after everyone left?" Bo demanded, his eyes studying her.

"Well—yes, but . . . " Kody mumbled, confused.

Why is he asking me that? she wondered, her heart starting to pound.

"That guard said he found you here last night," Bo continued, staring at her through his blue glasses.

"Yeah. Well—I was here," Kody said. "I was in the house, but—"

"You weren't out here in the back?" Bo demanded.

Kody suddenly realized why he was questioning her. He thinks I stayed late to loosen the thing that catches the camera!

"Bo—you don't think—" Her voice caught in her throat.

Bo uttered an unhappy sigh. "I don't know *what* to think, Kody. I just can't believe this happened. I—"

He stopped as uniformed paramedics ran across the yard, carrying metal cases of equipment. Three crew members were leading them to Joanna.

Several feet behind Bo, Kody saw the security guard staring accusingly at her.

This is crazy! Kody thought. Totally crazy!

Why would I mess with the camera?

Why?

"We'll talk later," Bo said, wiping sweat from his forehead with the sleeve of his sweatshirt.

"They're looking at a heavy-duty lawsuit," Kody heard someone say behind her.

"Let's just hope the girl lives," another voice added.

Her mind spinning, Kody turned and started to make her way toward the house.

But Bo came running up beside her. "Just one more question," he asked breathlessly. "Did you *know* that Persia was supposed to be on camera first this morning?"

"Huh?" Kody's mouth dropped open. "I don't understand."

"Well, you and Persia had that fight yesterday

evening," Bo replied, his cheeks pink. "And then the guard caught you hanging around late. I don't want to believe that you—well . . ." His voice trailed off.

"Then *don't* believe it!" Kody cried. "It's so *horrible,* Bo! I couldn't do anything like that. I wouldn't even know how! I—I don't know anything about cameras!"

"Okay, okay." Bo patted her shoulder. "I'm out of line. I apologize. I'm just totally whacked by this. I mean, I'm out of my head. I'm sorry. Really."

A crew member called frantically to Bo. Bo gave Kody a fretful wave, then hurried away.

Feeling dazed, Kody walked slowly toward the house.

I've got to get away from here, she thought.

Again she saw the camera sliding down, heard the horrifying *crack* as it slammed into Joanna's face.

How could Bo accuse me? Kody asked herself, feeling her anger rise.

So *what* if Persia and I have had some problems? Does that make me a *murderer?*

How could he think I'd loosen the bolts on the camera catch so it would smash into Persia?

How could he accuse me of anything like that?

Without realizing it, Kody had entered the house through the back door and was in the kitchen. She shook her head hard, as if trying to shake away her angry thoughts, and glanced around.

She half expected to see Mrs. Nordstrom bending over the sink, scrubbing away. But the kitchen was empty.

Through the window Kody watched medics hurry toward the street. They had Joanna on a stretcher, covered in a heavy blanket despite the morning heat. Joanna's arms were crossed over the blanket. Her face covered in blood-soaked bandages.

Is she alive? Kody wondered with a shudder.

Is she going to live?

She quickly turned away from the window, swallowing hard, trying to force down her nausea. Her throat felt achingly dry.

She shut her eyes and gripped the edge of the kitchen counter, struggling to steady herself, to calm her racing heart.

"Did you know Persia was going to be first?"

Bo's question repeated itself in her ears.

Kody opened her eyes. Where *is* Persia anyway? she wondered. How could Persia ignore all the screams and cries that followed the horrible accident?

Accident.

The word clung to Kody's mind.

Accident. It *could* have been an accident—couldn't it?

And then she had the horrifying answer. No. There *are* no accidents at 99 Fear Street. No accidents in this house.

Only evil. Deliberate evil.

Letting out a choked sob, Kody spun away from the counter. She took a few shaky steps across the kitchen, and then noticed the narrow streak of light across the linoleum.

Raising her eyes from the floor, she saw that the

refrigerator door was half open. A long rectangle of yellow light poured out from inside.

Weird, Kody thought.

The appliances in the kitchen are all props. Why is the refrigerator plugged in?

Crossing the room, she grabbed the door handle and started to push it closed. But her curiosity made her stop to peek inside.

Peering into the golden glow, Kody saw empty shelves.

Except for the object in the back of the top shelf that made her gasp.

A human head.

Blond hair. A green mouth, green as moldy bread, set in a twisted smile. Blue eyes staring blankly out at Kody.

Kody recognized the face at once.

Cally.

Cally's head!

Chapter 12

Kody's terrified screams brought several people running.

She heard the back door swing open. Heard heavy footsteps clambering over the floor. Heard muffled cries of surprise.

And then Kody felt Bo's gentle but firm hand pulling her away from the open refrigerator, out of the harsh yellow light.

"Kody—what?" he demanded softly. "What frightened you?"

A young red-haired woman—one of Bo's assistants —lifted the head out of the refrigerator. Holding it carefully in both hands, she held it up in front of her. "Is this what frightened you?"

Kody nodded, turning her head so that she wouldn't have to stare into the blue eyes.

"We put it in there to harden," Bo told her, still holding on to her trembling shoulders. "It's a model, Kody. The prop department brought it in this morning."

"What is her problem?" Kody heard someone whisper near the door.

"Did she think it was a real head?" someone else asked in a hushed voice.

"You've had a very upsetting morning," Bo told Kody. He signaled for the others to leave. The assistant replaced the head on the shelf and closed the refrigerator.

When everyone had left the room, Bo turned back to Kody. "We're all totally freaked by—by what happened. We all feel edgy. We all feel terrible about this morning. But we can't go over the edge," he said, eyeing her sternly. "I have a movie to make, and I'm going to make it, Kody. No matter what, I'm going to get this picture made."

"But it—it just looked so real," Kody murmured weakly. "I came back here to see my sister. And—there she was. And—"

Bo studied Kody for a moment. "Kody, I want you to go lie down in your trailer."

"But, Bo—!" Kody started to protest.

He raised a hand to silence her. "I'm afraid that coming back to this house has shaken you badly," he said, continuing to speak in a low, soothing tone. "That and the accident this morning . . ."

He turned and opened the refrigerator door. He reached onto the shelf and pulled out the head, smoothing the blond hair behind the face.

Kody stared once again at the sickening green lips, the lifeless blue eyes.

"It's not a real head. It's a model, Kody," Bo said, speaking very slowly, as if instructing a two-year-old. He raised it higher. "See?"

Kody nodded.

"Please," Bo said, sliding the head back into the refrigerator. "Go to your trailer. Okay? Rest. You'll be fine. Really."

"Okay," Kody replied uncertainly.

"We need you on this picture," Bo said, his eyes still studying her. "I need you. And I need you alert and in good shape. So, try real hard to get it together—okay?"

"I'll try," Kody told him.

She followed him out the kitchen door. Bo headed toward the crew members, who were working intently on the boom camera. Kody began to follow the driveway down to the street.

She had taken only a few steps when she heard Persia's scornful words, deliberately spoken loudly enough for Kody to hear. "I guess Kody just can't take all the stress," Persia was gloating to one of her assistants. "She isn't a pro, after all."

Well, well, Kody—so freaked out?

Did that little head frighten you, poor thing?

From the living room window, Cally's ghost

watched Kody trudge down the driveway to the long, tan trailer parked across the street.

My poor sister is terribly upset, Cally thought gleefully.

Kody, did it really upset you to see my head in the fridge?

I should be dead, right? Dead and gone. I shouldn't be popping up in the kitchen like that—should I!

Cally tilted her head back in a scornful laugh.

You said you came back to find me, Kody. You said you came back to keep your promise.

But when you *did* find me, what happened?

You totally freaked—didn't you, kid!

That's because you're a liar, Kody. That's because you didn't really come back to find your dead, dead sister.

You came back to become a movie star.

Only things aren't off to a good start, are they?

Someone got her pretty face bashed in, and—guess what, Kody? A lot of people out there think *you* were responsible.

That's because no one would suspect a ghost could loosen a few bolts. Am I right? No one would ever suspect a ghost.

Well, dear sister, the bad news is that this morning was just the beginning.

I'm afraid things aren't going to go right on your movie, Kody. I'm afraid there might be a lot of tragic accidents.

A lot.

What choice do I have, after all?

I mean, I can't really let you become a big movie star, can I? You made a promise to come back, to find me.

Well, maybe it's time, Kody.

Maybe it's time right now. No time like the present. Isn't that the old expression?

Well, okay. You can keep your promise now, Kody.

Here I come.

The morning sun beamed down on the metal trailer top, heating it like an oven. Desperate for some fresh air, Kody rolled a window open, but there was little breeze.

She squeezed behind the small Formica table and stared down at the fruit plate and blueberry muffin she had picked up at the caterers' table.

Why did I take this stuff? she asked herself. I have no appetite.

Kody's stomach felt as if it were tied in a knot. Her throat still throbbed, dry and achy. She took a sip from a bottle of water she had also picked up from the table.

She carried the water with her as she slumped onto the low couch. The leather felt warm and sticky under her. A fly buzzed noisily, banging its body against the windowpane.

Maybe I should quit, she thought sadly, raising her legs onto the couch cushion and stretching out. She rubbed the cool water bottle over her burning forehead.

Maybe I should quit before I go crazy, Kody thought.

Maybe everyone already thinks I'm crazy.

Maybe everyone already thinks I'm some kind of murderer!

She sighed and shut her eyes, covering them with one arm.

I thought so long and hard about doing this movie. I talked to Mom and Dad about it for months and months.

I was so sure I'd made the right decision.

But now . . .

She heard the tapping at the trailer door, but ignored it.

At first she thought it was just the creaking of the trailer.

But then she recognized the rhythm of the soft knocking.

Tap tap tap.

Silence.

Then: *tap tap tap.*

This time Kody didn't delay.

The grip of terror tightening every muscle, she forced herself to her feet.

And as the final tap sounded, she dove to the door and pushed it open.

Chapter 13

"Rob!" Kody cried, her voice revealing her shock.

"Hi." He stood on the bottom step, one hand resting on the slender railing. The bright sunlight made his auburn hair glow. He peered up at her, his expression serious.

"Rob—I thought—"

What *did* I think? Kody asked herself. That it was my dead sister knocking on the door?

Maybe I really *am* crazy!

"Just wondered how you were doing," Rob said.

"Okay, I guess." She backed up, motioning for him to come in.

He climbed the steps quickly and lowered his head

as he stepped into the narrow trailer. "Bad morning, huh?" he muttered. "Did you hear anything about Joanna? Is she—?"

Before Rob could finish, Kody threw her arms around him and pressed her mouth against his. "Hold me," she whispered. "I need you to hold me." Then she kissed him again.

Kody had never done anything like that in her life.

Cally had always been the bold one, the aggressive one, the one who took action. Kody had always stood back enviously and watched Cally as Cally made sure she got everything she wanted.

But now Kody had acted on impulse, had acted because she felt so strange, so frightened, so—needy.

Rob didn't seem to mind. As she lowered herself to the couch, he dropped down beside her, wrapping his arms around her waist, and kissed her, kissed her . . .

They were still wrapped in each other's arms as the door swung open and a figure stepped quickly into the trailer, clearing her throat loudly.

"I guess you didn't hear me knocking," Persia said.

Kody pulled back from Rob with a start. Rob leaped to his feet, his mouth wide open.

Persia laughed. "Well, Kody," she said coldly, "you're certainly learning how to succeed in the movies."

Rob glared at her angrily. "What's your problem, Persia? What do you want?"

"Bo says we're breaking for the day. The girl died,"

Persia told them matter-of-factly. "The police are all over the place. Investigating."

"You mean Joanna?" Kody asked, swallowing hard.

"I didn't know her name," Persia replied. "Anyway, your car is waiting if you want it. *Ciao.*" She backed out of the trailer and closed the door.

Kody turned back to Rob. "That's horrible news," she whispered, feeling a chill down her back as she shut her eyes and saw the camera ramming into Joanna's face again. "I—I can't believe it."

Rob wrapped his arms around Kody's waist and hugged her tight.

When Kody arrived at 99 Fear Street the next morning, she knew immediately that things were not back to normal. Two black and white police cars were parked at the bottom of the driveway where the caterers' truck usually stood. There were no production workers scurrying around, preparing for a morning shoot.

Warily, Kody entered the house and stepped into the living room. To her surprise, the room was filled with people.

"There you are," Bo called to her. Dressed in his usual gray sweatshirt and baggy chinos, he stood in front of the mantel. He didn't smile. He motioned with his clipboard for Kody to join the others.

Kody found Rob leaning against the back wall. She walked over to stand beside him. He gave her a solemn nod. "Bo called a meeting," he whispered.

The room was quiet. People whispered to one another or sat staring at Bo. No one smiled or laughed.

After a few more crew members found places on the floor in front of the couch, Bo cleared his throat loudly and stepped forward to speak.

"As you all know, we have had a tragic accident," he began.

Is he staring at *me?* Kody wondered, leaning close to Rob. It was hard to see Bo's eyes through the blue glasses.

"Because of the strange nature of Joanna's death," Rob continued, "the local police—"

He stopped and raised his eyes to the doorway. Kody turned to see a young man with long, dark hair and a dark mustache poke his head into the room. The man carried a red metal toolbox.

"I'm going down to the basement now, Mr. Montgomery," the man told Bo.

"Thank you," Bo replied, frowning at the interruption.

Kody gasped loudly.

She recognized the man. "Mr. Hankers!" she cried.

He had already disappeared from the doorway.

"That man is here to help us with our rat problem," Bo announced.

"You mean my agent is down there?" Persia joked.

A few people chuckled. Others murmured unhappily about the rats.

"Mr. Hankers has assured me the problem will be dealt with quickly," Bo said. "But until he finishes his work, I'd advise all crew members to take care when going down there."

"Are you okay?" Rob whispered to Kody, his features tight with concern.

Kody nodded. "I—I recognized that man," she explained. "He worked for us. We had a rat problem too."

Rob nodded. "No way I'm going down in the basement," he whispered. "I *hate* rats."

Bo continued talking, holding his clipboard down at his side, gesturing with his free hand.

But Kody didn't hear his words. She was thinking about Mr. Hankers. He had been the man her father had hired to deal with the rat problem two years earlier. How strange to see him again.

How strange to see Mr. Hankers and Mrs. Nordstrom still working in the house two years later. It was as if time had stood still.

Aren't they afraid to come here? Kody wondered.

After all that happened in this house, aren't they afraid to step inside?

Is Cally still here too?

Will I find her?

Kody believed in ghosts. The rest of her family had always teased her about it. But after Cally's death, Kody wanted to believe even more than before.

She *wanted* Cally's ghost to be in the house.

She *wanted* to find Cally, to have one last talk with her. Kody wanted Cally to know that she had kept her promise.

Are you here, Cally? Kody thought, gazing around the crowded, somber living room.

Are you here watching us?

If you are, please let me know.

Please . . .

The gentle hand on Kody's shoulder made her jump.

Chapter 14

"How are you doing?" Bo asked. Then he saw her jump. "Sorry, Kody. I didn't mean to startle you." He kept his hand on her shoulder. I can't believe how tense she is, Bo thought.

"Sorry. I was just thinking about—things," Kody told him.

Bo wanted to comfort Kody. He felt guilty about the way he had accused her the day before. He knew he had to calm her down so the picture could continue.

This picture will continue—no matter how many freak accidents slow things down, Bo vowed to himself.

"We're all really upset," Bo told her. "I was watching you while I was talking. I got the feeling you didn't hear a word I said."

He watched Kody blush and felt bad for her. She was having a rough time.

"I think we'll all feel better when the police end their investigation and we begin shooting," Bo said to her and Rob. "I hope to start tomorrow morning."

He clapped Rob on the back. "I want to do the attic scene first. You know. You and Kody stuck in the green goo. You can read over the script today, since we're not shooting."

"There isn't much to read," Rob replied. "Kody and I mainly do a lot of screaming."

"I want to block it out first thing," Bo told him, scribbling a note on his clipboard. "I have some ideas for camera angles to make it more interesting."

"Why are we shooting green goo in the attic? And why is Rob in the scene?" Kody asked, narrowing her eyes at Bo. "Actually, it was Cally and I. We were in the bathroom when the green goo came pouring out of the faucet."

"I know," he told her. "But the bathroom is too cramped. The attic will be much more dramatic."

"At least we'll be upstairs," Rob said, smiling. "As far away from the basement as possible." He shuddered. "I really hate rats."

"Yeah, me too." Bo nodded agreement. "That's one reason I want to start in the attic. We'll be safe up there."

I like Rob, Bo found himself thinking. Good attitude. Good poise. He gazed at Kody through his blue lenses. Maybe I should replace her now, he thought. Maybe if I beg the studio, they'll let me talk to a real actress.

He turned to say something else to Kody, but Persia stepped between them, her dark eyes flashing angrily. "Hey, Bo—how about a little quality time for me? After all, it was *my* stand-in who died. I mean—I just keep thinking, it could have been *me!*"

Bo felt like laughing in her face. Actors were all the same, he thought. So needy. So jealous of his attention.

"Why, of course, Persia dear," he said softly. He put his arm around Persia's shoulders and led her away, talking soothingly to her.

"Do you *believe* her?" Kody asked Rob, watching Bo lead Persia away.

"Hey, I've lived in L.A. my whole life," Rob replied. "I believe her."

Crew members huddled in small groups, talking about Joanna, the police investigation, and what it all meant for the movie. Kody saw the special effects guys heading up to the attic to prepare for the next day's shoot.

"I rented a car," Rob told her. "A Mustang convertible. Since we're not working today, why don't we take a long drive?"

Kody smiled at him. "You're a life saver!" she declared, taking his hand. "Let's go."

They climbed into the little car and drove north along the highway that led out of Shadyside. Through small towns and past miles and miles of farms. The green fields seeming to stretch on forever.

With the top down, Kody slumped low in the seat, enjoying the warmth of the sun on her face, letting the wind flutter her blond hair behind her.

Neither of them spoke much. It felt good just to drive, to be moving, moving farther and farther away from 99 Fear Street and its dark horrors.

They had lunch at a diner built from an old railroad car. Rob told her stories about growing up with a father in the movie business. "Sometimes it was great," he told her. "We never had to worry about money, and my parents gave me everything I wanted."

"But sometimes it wasn't so great," Rob admitted. "They gave me lots of stuff, but they were never around much. I mean, they didn't spend a lot of time with me. Sometimes I felt as if I were just one of my parents' possessions. They'd trot me out at parties and show me off. It was like, 'Look, we own one of *these* too!' "

Kody didn't have to tell Rob about her life. He already knew a lot of it.

She sat back in the booth and listened intently as he talked. It felt so good not to be thinking about the movie, about the tragedy of the day before—about Cally.

It was evening as they drove back to Shadyside. The wind carried a chill. Low clouds had rolled over the sun and were threatening rain.

Kody guided Rob to a spot called River Ridge, a

high cliff overlooking the Conononka River. It was a popular makeout spot for students at Shadyside High, Kody knew. But early in the evening, with the clouds threatening rain, the Mustang was the only car in sight.

As soon as he shut off the engine, Rob leaned over and kissed her. Then he wrapped Kody in a hug. They held on to each other for the longest time.

Neither of them moved.

Neither of them whispered.

Neither of them wanted to let go.

What a beautiful day this was, Kody thought. I feel so relaxed now, so . . . peaceful.

When the rain started to fall, softly at first, then as a hard, steady downpour, Rob jumped out and pulled up the top. He was drenched by the time he climbed back in the car.

He kissed her, a long, rain-wet kiss. Then he whispered, "Let's go back to my room and rehearse."

Kody started to say yes—then realized she didn't have her script. "I left it in my trailer," she told him, wiping raindrops off his forehead with her hand.

"We can share mine," he told her.

She shook her head. "It's better if I have mine. I like to make notes on it. Just drop me at the trailer, okay? I'll get the script. Then we can go to your room and rehearse."

Rob obediently started the car, and they drove down along the river, through a nice-looking neighborhood of big houses and wide, well-cared-for lawns, past the high school, toward Fear Street.

The rain came down harder as they turned onto Fear Street. The wind picked up, howling around the small car, making the old trees on both sides of them shiver and bend. In the headlights, the rain seemed to be blowing sideways.

Rob slowed when the movie company trailers came into view. The trailers were all dark, rainwater streaming down them.

Kody glanced up at the house. It was dark too, except for a flicker of light in the first-floor front window.

Probably the guard, she thought.

"I'll be right out," Kody told Rob, reaching for the door handle.

"Don't get wet," he joked.

She leaped out of the car and ran, in the sharp light of the headlights, the few steps to her trailer. The rain instantly soaked through her T-shirt and felt cold and tingly in her hair.

She struggled to open the trailer door. Stepping into the darkness, she shivered and wiped rainwater from her eyes and forehead.

The door slammed behind her. The wind howled, making the trailer shake.

Kody clicked on the overhead light.

The script. There it was on the low leather couch.

She bent to pick it up.

The rain pounding on the metal trailer roof sounded like a steady roar of thunder.

But over the drumming, she heard a knocking at the door.

Three taps.

Rob?

Why would Rob get out of the car?

Was it just the wind?

Holding the script away from her so she wouldn't get it wet, Kody listened.

Tap tap tap.

Silence.

Then: *Tap tap tap.*

Not the wind.

Not the patter of windswept rain against the door.

Swallowing hard, Kody made her way to the door. And pushed it open.

And stared into the curtain of rain at the darkness.

No one? No one there?

Kody rolled up the script to help keep it dry. She squinted into the hard rain, searched for the Mustang's headlights.

And realized the light was gone.

"Rob?" she called. Not loud enough, she realized, to be heard over the steady rumble of rain against the trailers, against the pavement.

Where was the car? Had he pulled up ahead to park at the curb?

She stepped out of the trailer, closing the door behind her. The wind blew her wet hair against her face. Sweeping it back with her free hand, she searched for Rob's car.

Not there.

Her heart began to pound as she stepped off the bottom step. She felt cold water against her ankle, glanced down, saw the deep puddle she had stepped in.

"Rob? Where are you?" she called.

He wouldn't leave her in the rain. He wouldn't.

And then, as the wind howled through the shivering trees, Kody heard the whisper: *"Kody—here I am."*

"No!" Kody covered her mouth with her free hand. The cold rain washed over her. "No!"

Just the wind.

Just the wind and my imagination.

"Kody—I am here. Kody—I am with you."

Kody held her breath, struggled to see through the dark, shifting curtains of rain.

It's Rob, she thought suddenly. Rob playing some sort of cruel joke.

But as the whispers rose over the wind once again, Kody recognized her sister's voice.

"Kody—I am with you. Kody—it's me. Cally."

"Cally? Is it really you?" Kody screamed. She felt all her muscles tighten. She felt as if her chest were about to burst.

Happiness. Excitement. Fear. All at once. All mixed together.

"Cally!" she cried. "Cally—I can't see you! Where are you?"

Chapter 15

The rain swept down, the wind howled, and the voice whispered again, *"Follow me. Follow me, Kody."*

The trailer shook behind her. Kody watched a jagged bolt of lightning crack over the trembling trees.

"Follow me—now!"

Water ran down Kody's face. She squinted through the raindrops, trying to catch a glimpse of her twin sister. "Wh-where are you?" she stammered. "I can't see you, Cally!"

"Follow me. I am with you. Follow me now."

The script fell from Kody's hand into the deep puddle at her feet. As she began to follow the voice toward the house, a strong gust of wind rushed forward to meet her. It pushed her back as if trying to keep her away.

But Kody knew she had to follow her sister's whispered commands.

Kody had no choice. This was why she came back. She had made a promise to Cally. And no wind or rain or bolts of lightning would stop her from keeping that solemn promise.

Bending against the swirling wind, Kody made her way through sheets of rain up the gravel driveway. "Cally, are you still here? Is it really you?" she shouted over the thunderclap that shook the trees.

No reply.

Rainwater poured through a broken gutter over the porch, splashing noisily onto the walk. Orange light flickered in the rain-smeared living room window.

"Cally? Are you here?"

Again Cally's voice rose on the wind, a whisper, a faint beckoning whisper that Kody had to struggle to hear over the roar of the rain.

"This way, Kody. Come this way."

Kody stepped around the splashing water from the broken gutter. Onto the porch. Out of the wind.

With a hard shiver, she pushed open the front door. And stepped into the warmth of the house.

"This way, Kody." The voice sounded stronger in the hallway, out of the wind and rain.

"Cally! It really *is* you!" Kody forgot her fright as her excitement took over, the excitement of this impossible reunion.

"This way. Don't stop."

"Cally—I saw you in that window," Kody called out to her. "After you died, I saw you watching from the window. I promised I'd come back. Did you hear me then, Cally? Did you hear my promise?"

Silence.

Kody realized she couldn't stop shivering. She pushed both hands back through the soaked tangles of her hair, sending a shower of raindrops to the carpet. Then she wrapped her arms around herself, struggling to stop the cold, wet chills.

"Cally? Where are you? Can I see you?"

"Follow me, Kody. I want to see you too."

"Cally—it sounds like you!" Kody cried, her voice trembling from the shivers that convulsed her body. "It really does!"

Why can't I warm up? Kody wondered, following the voice to the back hall. Why can't I stop shivering?

"I've missed you so much, Cally," she told her sister. "I thought about you every day. Every single day. Somehow, you were always there. Always beside me. Always in my mind."

"I thought about you too," the voice replied. But without any warmth. *"I thought about you too, Kody."* The words came out icy and hard.

Kody hesitated at the door to the basement. "Are you down there, Cally?"

No reply.

Kody raised both hands and wiped rainwater from her forehead and eyebrows. If only I could stop shaking! she told herself.

She pulled open the basement door and peered

down the dark stairs. Pale light reflected off the gray stone basement walls. "Are you down there, Cally?"

"Yes, I'm down here. Come down, Kody. Come and find me."

Holding tightly to the railing, Kody began to lower herself down the steep, narrow steps. Her sneakers squished on each creaking stair.

She stopped halfway down, remembering the rats.

"Cally? Are you really down here? Can I see you?"

"Come and find me. Hurry!" the voice urged sharply.

Yes. Cally was down in the basement.

Kody's temples throbbed. Her legs felt weak as she made her way to the basement floor.

Shadows moved in the pale light. The gray walls appeared to tilt as Kody took a step, then another. "Cally?" Her voice came out small and frightened. "Can I see you?"

A scraping sound. Close by.

Was it a rat?

Rain pounded against the small windowpane above Kody's head at ground level. "Cally?" Kody took another step into the basement. She saw several large wooden storage crates piled one on top of the other over the floor.

A wisp of light flickered behind a tall tower of crates.

"Cally—are you back there?" Kody asked meekly.

Silence.

The light flickered.

Something scuttled across the concrete floor.

The wind splattered rain against the tiny basement window.

"Here I am, Kody. I've waited so long for you."

"Oh, Cally!" Kody exclaimed, her voice trembling with emotion. With a hard shiver, she rushed toward the flickering light—but her leg struck something hard, and she stumbled over it.

A low wooden crate.

"Ow!" Kody cried out, landing hard on one elbow.

Pain shot up her arm and down her right side.

Rubbing her elbow, she pulled herself up to her knees. "Cally? Are you here?"

Staring toward the cartons, still on her knees, Kody saw a dark shadow roll across the floor.

As the shadow rolled over her, Kody started to scream.

But a hand clamped itself tightly over her mouth.

Chapter 16

"Shhhhhh."

She felt hot breath on her cheek.

She wanted to scream. But the hand held on tightly.

Kody tried to duck away. But she felt so panic-stricken, her muscles wouldn't cooperate.

She lowered herself to the floor in surrender.

The hand loosened its grip.

She turned and gazed into Bo's stubbled face.

He had a finger raised to his lips. His eyes flared excitedly in the eerie, pale glow of his penlight.

"Kody—what are you doing down here?" he whispered.

"You—you scared me to death!" she managed to choke out angrily. She jumped to her feet and crossed her arms protectively over her chest as she glared at him.

"Answer my question," he insisted, his eyes studying her, her wet clothes, her disheveled hair. "What are you doing down here?"

"I—I—" Kody stammered. How could she explain that she had followed her sister's ghost? "What are *you* doing down here, Bo?" she demanded instead.

"I have a right to be down here," he said softly, still studying her. "I have work to do for the production. But, Kody—"

"You're here all by yourself? So late?" she insisted.

"Kody, I work very late hours. It's part of being the director. But I really have to ask you to explain yourself," Bo said, his expression growing stern.

"I—well . . ."

"The security guard said he caught you in the house the night before last," Bo said, rubbing his stubbled jaw thoughtfully. "And now, here you are again. I don't want to believe anything bad about you, Kody. But I have to know what's going on."

"I can't really explain," Kody started to say.

He shook his head. "You *have* to explain," he told her. He took her hand and squeezed it between his. "Ooh. You're so cold, Kody. Cold and wet."

"I know. I was out in the rain. I—"

"Perhaps we should get out of this house," Bo suggested. "Perhaps we should go back to the hotel, and you can tell me why we keep finding you in places where you don't belong."

He held on to her hand. But Kody realized it wasn't a friendly gesture. He was trying to frighten her.

He suspected her of doing something wrong, of being up to no good. And he was trying to intimidate her, to frighten her into confessing.

"Should we talk back at the hotel?" he repeated, holding her hand tightly.

Kody hesitated.

"This picture is very important to me, Kody," Bo said, squeezing her hand. "It's very important to my career. I won't let anything ruin it for me. Anything—or anyone. I'm a very understanding guy. I always try to think the best of people. But finding you down here—"

"It's hard to explain," Kody interrupted. "But my sister—"

She stopped when she saw the light flash on the label on the wooden crate that Bo was leaning on. She squinted at it to make sure she had read it correctly. Then she saw the same label on the crate beneath it.

"Bo!" she cried, unable to hide her surprise. "These boxes—they're filled with explosives!"

His expression changed instantly. His eyes narrowed, and his mouth tensed. "Kody," he whispered, leaning toward her menacingly, "I'm really sorry you saw these."

Chapter 17

Kody drew back. "Bo—you're frightening me. Why are you staring at me like that?"

His expression seemed to soften in the dim light. "I'm sorry," he said. "It's just that—you weren't supposed to see this." He patted the top of the wooden crate gently.

"But I don't understand," Kody choked out. "So many boxes of explosives."

"I don't want anyone to know," Bo repeated, scratching his hair, tugging back his ponytail. "It's supposed to be a secret, Kody. I just moved these crates down here tonight."

She lowered her eyes to the label on the crate. The first word up at the top was DANGER.

"I don't want the cast to know the ending of the film," Bo said, leaning on the crate. "That's why I didn't pass out the last ten pages of the script."

"You mean—?" Kody started to ask.

He pulled off the blue glasses. "I'm going to blow up the house," he revealed. "It's going to be an incredible explosion. I mean, I'm really going to do it. *Boooom!*" He gestured with both hands, the light weaving drunkenly.

Kody stared at him, startled by his sudden enthusiasm.

"But you've got to swear to keep it a secret," Bo said, lowering his voice. "I want genuine surprise on the faces of my actors. I want to see *real* horror on their faces when the house goes up. Do you understand?"

Kody nodded. "Yes, but—"

She heard scuttling sounds behind her in the darkness. Scratching. A soft hiss.

The sounds sent chills down her back.

I have to get out of here, she thought. I have to get back to the hotel and into some dry clothes.

"I won't tell anyone, Bo," she promised. "Really. My lips are sealed." She ran a hand across her mouth in a zipper motion.

He studied her in the low light. "It doesn't matter that you know the ending," he said, thinking out loud. "You're Cally. You're already dead when the house blows up."

Cally! Kody thought. Cally led me down here. Her voice . . .

"Of course, Cally is still in the house," Bo continued, staring hard at her. "You blow up in the house. Hey—maybe we see you explode too. You know. Your head shoots up in the air. Your arms and legs go flying in different directions. . . ."

Kody let out a low cry.

"Sorry," Bo said quickly. "You have too many real memories here, huh?"

Kody nodded. "Yes. My sister—"

He reached out and took her hand again. "If you're having trouble dealing with all this, Kody, I could make a cast change. Persia is ready to step into your role, as you know. You could take a smaller part. You could play yourself. Then the pressure would be off, and—"

"No!" Kody interrupted shrilly. "No! No way! I *know* Persia is dying to take my part away from me. But I'm playing Cally, Bo. I'm playing the part. It—it's very important to me."

"Okay. Okay." He backed off. "I'm just trying to understand you, Kody." His expression hardened. "You still haven't explained why you're down here. I explained why *I'm* here. I was checking to make sure these explosives were stored properly. But I still haven't heard why—"

"It's because of my sister!" Kody blurted out.

Bo's mouth dropped open. He started to say something, but changed his mind and waited for Kody to continue.

"Cally called to me," Kody told him. "Outside. I heard her voice. She told me to follow her. She led me into the house. I mean, her *voice* led me. And—and—"

Kody stopped. "You don't believe what I'm saying, right? You think I'm totally messed up."

Bo shook his head. "Go with it," he said enthusiastically. "I like it. Maybe we can add it to the script. You know. The scene when you come home after Cally's funeral. Go on, Kody. Go with it."

"I'm not making it up!" Kody screamed, feeling herself lose control. "It's *real,* Bo! It's not part of the movie!"

She heard the soft scuttling, the scratching sounds again.

Closer this time. And in front of her. Somewhere in front of her.

"Finish the explanation," Bo insisted. "The voice led you down here and—"

They both saw the dark form leap off the top of the crate.

A fat gray rat.

Kody saw its red eyes first. Then its pointed teeth.

Before she could raise her hands to protect herself, she heard its shrill hiss—as it leaped for her throat.

Chapter 18

Kody uttered a loud shriek and stumbled backward.

The rat, its teeth bared, sailed at her.

Missed.

Hit the hard floor with a disgusting *plop*.

Momentarily stunned, it gazed up hungrily at Kody. Its long, pink tail twitched back and forth over the floor.

It pulled itself to its feet.

And before the rat could leap again, Kody kicked out at it.

Her wet sneaker caught the rat in the belly.

It let out a startled shriek as it went flying into the wooden crate. Then it dropped heavily to the floor and scuttled away, its nails scratching over the concrete.

"Ohhh." Kody uttered a sigh of relief. Her heart thudded loudly in her chest. She could still feel the heavy rat against the toe of her sneaker, still hear the soft *plop* the ugly creature made as it hit the floor.

She shut her eyes, trying to fight down the waves of nausea that rose from her stomach. And felt Bo's arm go around her shoulders.

"Come on," he whispered, guiding her to the stairs. "Let's get out of here."

Gratefully, Kody let him lead her out of the basement.

"I hired that guy to get rid of the rats," Bo muttered unhappily. "I thought he knew what he was doing. But I guess the job was too much for him."

Kody's legs trembled as she made her way up the steep, narrow stairs.

I've got to get out of this house, she told herself. I've got to get away from here. I've got to go someplace—safe.

"If one more disaster occurs on this picture . . ." Bo was saying. He shut the basement door tightly behind them. "This film is so important to me. If one more bad thing happens, I—I really don't know *what* I'll do!"

The ghost of Cally floated up from the basement in time to hear Bo's words.

Cally laughed to herself, a scornful snicker.

"One more bad thing?" she wondered. "One more bad thing? That can be arranged."

Cally watched her sister and the movie director hurry out the front door. She floated to the window and stared out at them as they made their way down the rain-puddled driveway to his car.

"One more bad thing?" Cally repeated, watching them drive away. "No problem, guys." A cruel smile crossed Cally's once-pretty face. "How about tomorrow?"

Chapter 19

"Ernie, you've double-checked everything?" Kody heard Bo ask the special effects person as she stepped into the attic, closing the door behind her.

"Checked, double-checked, triple-checked," Ernie reported, giving Bo a comical salute.

Kody liked Ernie. He was funny. He looked sort of like a squirrel, with short brown hair, pouchy cheeks, and two front teeth that stuck out.

He and Bo leaned against the attic wall, studying the black metal machine that Ernie christened the Goo Works.

In addition to the Goo Works, the attic room was cluttered with cameras, cables, and lights. The lights were already on, so bright they drowned out the morning sunlight beaming through the closed window.

Crew members huddled around the equipment, talking quietly, sipping from cardboard coffee cups, waiting for the shoot to begin.

Kody hesitated at the door. Bo and Ernie were concentrating so intently on their work, they hadn't noticed her come in.

Finally Bo turned around, and a smile crossed his face. "Right on time. How are you today, Kody? You look terrific. But how are you *underneath* the makeup?"

Kody smiled back at him. "Underneath the makeup, I'm a quivering mess!" she confessed. "It *is* my first day of shooting, after all."

"Hey, leave the quivering mess to me!" Ernie declared. "Quivering messes are my job." He patted the machine.

"Ernie is going to explain the goo machine as soon as Rob arrives," Bo said, studying his clipboard. "Remember, we rehearsed this scene back in L.A.?"

Kody nodded. "I have to scream a lot," she remembered.

"A lot," Bo agreed. "Hope you're in good voice this morning, dear."

The attic door opened and Rob entered. He greeted everyone cheerily and flashed Kody a warm smile as he walked over to her.

"Where *were* you last night?" Kody whispered. "Why did you drive away and leave me?"

"Huh?" Rob's face was confused. "You *told* me to go on without you. Don't you remember?"

"I *what?"* Kody cried, equally confused.

"You ran out to the car. You told me to leave. To go back to the hotel."

"I did *not!"* Kody whispered, very confused.

"But you did!" Rob insisted. "I never would've driven off if you hadn't told me to!"

"Let's get to work, kids," Bo scolded.

"Oh. Right. Sorry," Rob replied, blushing. "What's up?"

"You're going to be up—up to your knees in green goo," Bo told him. "Come over here, guys. I want to block this out quickly. Once the goo starts pumping, we have to get it right."

"That's for sure," Ernie added. "If we have to do a second take, it'll take *hours* to clean this stuff off the floor first."

"Better alert that cleaning woman we hired!" Bo joked. "Tell her she may be getting a lot of overtime."

Bo positioned Kody and Rob for the scene, moving them to spots marked in chalk on the floor, then checking with the camera operator to make sure they looked okay.

He instructed the crew to move some lights. Then he returned to Kody and Rob.

"A quick run-through, okay? You rehearsed this yesterday on your own, right?"

"Kind of," Kody lied. "I'm pretty sure I've got it."

Bo's eyes narrowed at her disapprovingly. "Kind of?"

"It's getting close to our break," Ernie called from behind the machine.

"Let's get started," Bo replied impatiently. He pointed down at the floor. "See those ducts? Don't stand on them," he instructed.

"Those are the goo ducts?" Rob asked.

Bo nodded. "Ernie has four of them hidden in the floor."

"When I throw the switch, the green stuff is going to come pouring up," Ernie told them. "Now, don't be surprised. It's going to come pumping up really fast."

"Be surprised," Bo corrected him. "Be very surprised, okay, kids?" He put a hand on Kody's shoulder. "I want you to be more than surprised when that goo starts flowing. I want you to be terrified, got it?"

"It's thick and it should be a little warm," Ernie told them. "It looks real lumpy, like oatmeal. But don't worry. It doesn't smell. It has no odor at all."

Kody let out a sigh of relief. Rob laughed, nervous laughter.

She felt glad that Rob was nervous too.

What if I mess up? she asked herself. They say it'll take hours to clean the floor so we can start again. If I mess up the scene, I'll be so embarrassed.

"If it's pumping right, it should rise up to your ankles in no time," Ernie explained.

"You don't notice it until then," Bo reminded them, flipping through green-tinted script pages on his clipboard. "Cally and Anthony have sneaked up to the attic to make out. You're standing there with your arms around each other, kissing passionately. We see the green gunk rising up from the floor. But you don't even feel it till it's practically to your knees."

"Then we scream in horror," Rob said. "And do we try to get to the door right away?"

"We have to see you struggle in the stuff," Bo instructed. "It's pulling you down, sucking you under. It's rising higher and higher, and you're trapped in it."

"How high is it going to rise?" Kody asked warily, staring down at the large, round duct at her feet.

Ernie laughed. "Don't worry. There's only enough goo in the machine to go up to your knees. And it's not really that sticky. Like I said, it's sort of like oatmeal. You won't have any trouble walking out of it when the scene is over."

"Now I understand why they gave me this yellow shirt. It's because it'll look good with the green!" Rob joked.

"I'm all in blue. I'm going to clash," Kody complained playfully.

"As you struggle, try to splash the stuff over each other," Bo instructed, ignoring their jokes. "Make it look good. You know. You're thrashing your arms frantically. You're struggling. Struggling. And the more you struggle, the more you get covered in the yucky stuff."

"What if I fall facedown in it?" Rob suggested. "You know. Just take a nosedive."

Bo shook his head. "It's not a comedy, Rob. If I wanted a comedy, we'd have a pie fight up here."

"I see where you're coming from," Rob replied seriously.

"I want to see the disgust on your faces," Bo told them, turning his gaze on Kody. "You're up to your knees in vomit, right? You've got to make the audience *feel* it. You've got to make them squirm like you're squirming. You've got to make them *smell* it!"

"Break, everyone!" a crew member called from the attic doorway.

The lights were shut off. The floorboards creaked under the weight of the workers as they hurried to the stairs. They took their breaks seriously.

"Hey, guys—back in fifteen!" Bo called to them. He turned to Kody and Rob. "You coming down? Want a muffin or something? Some coffee?"

Kody and Rob exchanged glances. "I'd rather stay up here and rehearse," Kody replied.

"Yeah. It'll be quiet. We can get it all worked out," Rob agreed.

Bo gave them a wave and hurried out the door.

Rob turned to Kody. "So? How are you feeling? You okay?"

She shrugged. "You help cool me out," she told him. "You're always making jokes, keeping it light. That helps a lot."

"I'm just covering up the fact that I'm in a total panic!" he exclaimed.

They both laughed.

"What part do you want to rehearse? Where do you want to start?" Rob asked.

She flashed him a teasing smile. "Why don't we start with this?" She moved close, swung her arms around his shoulders, and pulled his head down for a kiss.

When the kiss ended, she started to step away. But Rob pulled her close. "Not quite right," he said playfully. "I think we'd better rehearse it again."

"My lipstick—" Kody protested. "I'll have to go back to Makeup."

"Who cares?"

Rob started to kiss her again—when the attic door slammed.

Startled, they both turned to see who had come in.

No one there.

"Must be a breeze or something," Rob suggested. "Now, where were we?"

She raised both hands in front of her to keep him away. "Let's go over the lines, okay?" she asked.

Rob started to reply. But a sound against the wall made them both turn.

With a loud *click,* the lever on the side of the goo machine slid down.

The machine hummed softly, then louder as the pump started to churn.

"Hey—what's going on?" Rob cried.

Chapter 20

Kody jumped as warm green goo splashed up over her white sneakers.

"I—I don't believe this!" she cried. The thick green liquid was spouting up from all four ducts.

Something started up the machine, she realized. We've got to turn it off before it messes up the whole scene.

"Ow! It's *hot!*" Rob exclaimed as the green goo splashed the leg of his jeans.

Dodging around a spouting duct, her sneakers sliding over the chunky green liquid, Kody reached the machine first. She grabbed the lever and tried to tug it back up.

"Hey—!" she cried out when it wouldn't budge.

The machine chugged away.

Turning back, she saw the green goo spreading over the attic floor. It made a sickening plopping sound as it poured out from the four ducts.

Kody tried the lever again. No success.

Rob bent to help out. Kody stepped back to let him try his luck. He strained with both hands. "It—won't—move!" he cried. "I can't turn it off!"

"I thought Ernie said the stuff didn't smell!" Kody exclaimed, her face twisted in disgust. The foul odor brought back a flood of awful memories.

"Ooooh." The sour aroma invaded Rob's nose too. "It smells like really sour milk," he groaned.

Kody took a deep breath and held it, trying to stop the nausea that gripped her stomach.

Rob gave the lever one more hard pull with both hands, putting all his strength into it. "Aaaaagh!" He let out a cry of frustration and stepped back.

"Ow! The stuff *is* hot! It's burning hot!" Kody declared. She raised her knees high as she backed away. The green liquid bubbled and gurgled up over her sneakers.

"We've got to get Ernie and Bo!" Rob cried. "The lever is totally stuck."

Kody started to the attic door. "Ow! The machine—it must be broken! Why is the goo so hot?"

Her sneakers stuck. She struggled to raise them. She felt a stab of fear in her chest. "It—it's holding me down, Rob!"

"Me too!" he called, close behind her. He leaned his

weight forward, trying to move. "Ohhh, the putrid smell!"

Kody heard him cry out. She spun around in time to see him fall forward, his hands shooting out to break the fall.

"Ow!" He landed with a hard *splat.* Then raised his head, his eyes wide with fear. "I—I can't get up, Kody! It's holding me—holding me down!"

"Huh?" Kody let out a surprised cry. She turned back to him, her sneakers sliding in the hot green liquid.

The goo made a slapping sound as it washed over her ankles and spread onto the legs of her jeans.

She stretched out both hands, reached down for him.

"Hold on," Kody urged. "I've *got* you!"

She grabbed his hands. They were sticky with goo. Thick clots of it rolled down his bare arms, onto the front of his yellow T-shirt.

"Help me," Rob pleaded. "I really feel sick, Kody. I think I'm going to hurl."

She helped to pull him up. He grabbed her shoulder and hoisted himself to his feet. "Stop! You're smearing it all over me!" she cried.

The chunky green liquid rolled over the floor like ocean waves, rolled up under their jeans, halfway up their legs.

"Where is everyone?" Kody demanded. "Can't anyone hear the pump going? Can't anyone hear that the stupid machine started up?"

Rob didn't reply. He was concentrating on raising one foot, then the other, making his way slowly, with enormous effort, toward the attic door.

The sour aroma swept over Kody. She tried to breathe through her mouth. The gurgling, lapping green liquid rose higher, nearly to her knees. It burned her legs, clung to her jeans, splashed against her as she struggled to move.

Rob made it to the door first. Kody saw that his forehead dripped with sweat. His face was bright red. He was breathing hard from his efforts.

"Pull the door open!" Kody urged. "Quick, Rob. It's up to my knees!" She watched him grab the knob. His sticky hand slipped off it.

He wiped his hand on a dry patch on the side of his jeans and grabbed the doorknob again. He turned it and pulled.

Kody saw his face grow redder. "Hey—!" He let out a startled cry.

"Hurry, Rob!" she urged. "It's really burning me now! My legs are on fire!"

"Mine too!" he choked out. He tugged at the door.

She saw his feet slip on the thick, slimy surface.

He caught his balance by throwing his shoulder against the door. Then he pulled again, pulled until his face was nearly purple.

"Rob—what's wrong?" Kody called shrilly, struggling to reach him.

He turned back to her, his eyes wide with horror. "The door—" he cried. "It's *locked!*"

Chapter 21

"It *can't* be!" Kody cried.

The hot green liquid rolled against her legs, wave after sickening wave. She kept shifting her weight, lifting her legs high, struggling not to become stuck.

Rob tried the door again, pulling with all his strength. He screamed for help. There was no reply.

She saw his hands slip off the doorknob again, saw him stumble backward. The sticky green goo swept up against Rob's waist.

He turned to her, his features tight with fear. "Didn't Ernie say there was only enough goo to come up to our knees?"

Kody nodded. "It won't go much higher," she said,

trying to sound hopeful. "It'll turn off any second now."

But so far, everything Ernie had said had been wrong.

"They should be back from their break," Rob said, pounding with both fists on the attic door. "Where *are* they?"

He screamed again. Still no reply.

Kody was fighting hard. Trying to forget. But still remembering.

Remembering the horrors her family had faced in this frightening house. Remembering the night the disgusting green goo had poured down the bathroom walls.

Ernie's machine isn't pumping this green goo, she realized.

This is the evil of the house.

"Cally—are you here?" Kody called suddenly. "Cally?"

Rob's mouth dropped open. He leaned forward, pushed his legs up, trying to cross the swirling, seething sea of green to her. "Kody—are you okay?"

"Cally is here," Kody replied, her eyes darting around the room. "I can sense it."

"But, Kody—" Rob was pushed back by a high wave.

"Cally will help us, Rob," Kody assured him. "She's here. I know she is. And she will help us get out of here."

"Kody—please," Rob begged, struggling harder to

pull himself through the swirling hot liquid. "Take a deep breath. I'll get us out of here."

"You think I'm crazy—don't you," Kody accused him sadly. Turning away from him, she cupped her hands around her mouth and shouted, "Cally! Cally?"

"If it gets any higher, we can *swim* out!" Rob called.

"It's too thick to swim in," Kody replied grimly. She called to her sister again.

No reply.

The only sound in the room now was the gurgle and splash of the green liquid as it rose higher and higher.

"It—it's so gross!" Kody complained. "I can't move, Rob. I feel as if it's pulling me down into it."

"Stay on your feet," Rob ordered. "It can't get much higher—can it?"

They raised their arms to keep them out of the roiling goo, which had climbed waist-high. Thick chunks washed against their bodies, swirling in the steaming broth. The aroma grew stronger, choking them, sickening them, forcing them to breathe hard through their mouths.

"Cally? Cally—can you hear me?" Kody cried frantically. "Are you here? Can you help us?"

No reply.

"Your sister is dead, Kody," Rob said softly. "She can't help us now."

She's here, Kody told herself.

She's here. I know she is.

Why isn't she helping us?

Sweat poured down Kody's face. Her wet hair

matted against her forehead. "I feel as if I'm melting," she moaned, "melting right into it."

Rob didn't answer. He was wiping green chunks off the front of his T-shirt.

"Rob—it's getting higher," she said weakly. "Pretty soon, we won't be able to move."

Kody searched desperately around the room. "Hey—the window!" she cried. "Rob—that window leads out to the roof."

"All *right!"* Rob cried excitedly, his enthusiasm quickly fading. "What makes you think we can get over to it, Kody?"

"We *have* to!" Kody declared.

Leaning forward, pressing into the thick swirls of green, she started toward the window.

"It feels as if it's pushing me back," Rob called from behind her. "As if it's *deliberately* trying to keep me from the window."

"Keep going," Kody urged breathlessly. "Keep pushing."

"I—I don't think I can make it," he cried weakly. "I—I'm going to *drown* in this stuff."

"No!" She turned her head. "We're moving, Rob. We're almost there. Keep going. Don't give up."

"The smell—" he moaned. "I—feel—really . . ." His voice trailed off.

"Only a few more feet," Kody murmured. "A few more feet." She thrust her body forward, her arms outstretched.

The thick liquid swept against her, pushing her back, wave after hot wave.

But she kept her legs moving, kept pushing, pushing, pushing—

Until her outstretched palms pressed against the glass of the windowpane.

"Yes!" she cried triumphantly. "We're going to get out now, Rob! Hurry! We're going to get out!"

Her hands slid over the glass. She placed them on the window frame and pushed.

The window didn't budge.

She pushed harder.

Her feet slid out from under her. The hot green liquid splashed against her chest.

Regaining her balance, Kody checked the lock on top of the lower sash. Not locked.

She pushed up against the frame.

The window didn't budge. "It's stuck too," she managed to choke out.

She banged both fists furiously against the glass. "Let us out! Let us out!" she cried in shrill terror.

The hot, churning liquid had climbed over her waist.

With a desperate burst of strength, she turned to the left. Reached out. Grabbed a light tower, a slender metal frame that held two large lights.

Nearly losing her balance again, nearly slipping headfirst into the goo, she managed to raise the light tower into the air.

Holding it shakily over her head with both hands, she slammed it hard against the window glass.

The windowpane cracked. A spiderweb of cracks

spread over the glass. And then the glass dropped out onto the roof.

"Yes!" Kody cried happily, knocking the jagged shards out too.

Tossing the light tower behind her, she raised both hands to the windowsill. It took all of her remaining strength to lift herself out of the thick liquid.

Pulling until her knees rose to the sill, she half fell, half dived onto the flat shingle roof.

"Rob!" she called. "Hurry, Rob! We're out! We're okay!"

When he didn't reply, Kody felt dread tighten in the pit of her stomach. "Rob?" she called, her chest aching as she struggled to catch her breath.

"Rob?"

Sliding over the shingles, she crawled back to the window. Pressing both hands on the sill, she peered into the attic room.

"Nooooooo!" A horrified wail burst from deep inside her. "Rob—nooooooooo!"

Chapter 22

As the howls escaped her throat, Kody peered in at Rob. He floated lifelessly on the surface of the tossing liquid, his face buried in the goo, his arms sprawled straight out.

He was inches from the window. Inches from escape.

He probably tried to swim, Kody realized, and the disgusting liquid held him under.

"Rob? Rob?" She called to him without realizing it, unable to hear her voice over the pounding of her heart, over the pain of her thoughts.

And then, without thinking about it, in a blur of action Kody climbed onto the windowsill, lowered herself to her knees, took a deep breath—and leaned over the thick, swirling broth.

Stretched out both hands. Stretched them farther, leaning in as far as she could. Reached. Reached.

Grabbed Rob by the hair. And tugged his face out of the goo.

Are you still breathing? she wondered.

Please, Rob. Please be breathing. Please!

She had no choice. She had to lower herself back into the hot goo. Wrapping her hands under Rob's armpits, she swung him onto his back. The green slime clung to his face, to his clothes, to his hair.

Grabbing the windowsill with her left hand, she pulled Rob over the surface of the goo with her right.

I can't lift him out. But maybe I can slide him, she thought.

Please, Rob. Please be breathing.

She had to let go of him to hoist herself out of the deep liquid and back onto the windowsill. Then she turned back, bent to grab him with both hands. Tugged. Tugged until it felt as if her chest were about to burst.

She toppled backward as his body came sliding out onto the flat roof. She landed hard on her side, but ignored the pain and quickly scrambled back to him.

Please breathe. Please.

He lay sprawled on his back, his eyes shut, his body still.

Please. *Please!*

Kody pounded hard on his chest.

Please breathe. *Please breathe.*

She gasped in one deep breath after another. But her chest continued to ache.

Leaning over Rob, she frantically wiped green clots from around his mouth. Then she lowered her mouth to his and began giving him mouth-to-mouth.

"Ohhh." She let out a low moan as she tasted the sour green goo. It felt gritty against her lips. It tasted like rancid buttermilk.

But she lowered her mouth once again to his.

And breathed, pushing her breath into him, trying to ignore the sour taste.

Breathe.

Breathe.

Rob groaned.

Yes!

Breathe. Breathe.

He groaned again and blinked his eyes.

Kody raised her head, wiping a green clot from her chin.

Yes. Rob was breathing on his own now. Breathing noisily. But breathing.

Shutting her eyes, Kody said a silent prayer of thanks.

Then she turned away from Rob and started to vomit.

The next afternoon Bo furiously paced back and forth in the living room, talking in a high, excited voice. Kody shrank back on the couch against the wall. Why does he keep glaring at me like that? she wondered. As if what happened was my fault?

"I don't see how we can continue. This is a farce, Bo," Persia was saying from the other couch. One of her assistants brought her a Diet Coke in a tall glass.

"This movie will be made. We *have* to continue," Bo replied heatedly. "And fast."

He continued to pace, swinging the clipboard in one hand as he walked. "If I know Rob's father, he'll have the place swarming with lawyers in no time. He'll sue us for every penny the production has. He'll charge negligence—and he'll win."

"How *is* Rob?" Kody asked from the back of the room. She'd been calling the hospital all morning. But they wouldn't give her any information.

"The word from the hospital is that he's doing pretty well," Bo replied grimly. "He's in shock, they say. But he's going to be okay."

"We're *all* in shock," someone murmured.

"I can still smell that stuff," someone else said.

A few people turned to stare at Kody.

Do they expect me to still be covered in it or something? she wondered unhappily. Why is everyone gawking at me?

"Anyone see Ernie?" one of the prop crew asked.

The room fell silent. "Ernie is no longer with us," Bo replied finally. "I—uh—had no choice. I had to fire him." He swallowed hard. "Ernie and I were together a long time. But he—he nearly ruined the whole production with that stupid machine of his."

The room rumbled with whispers and surprised murmurs.

It wasn't Ernie's fault, Kody realized, crossing her

arms over her chest and sinking back into the armchair.

It wasn't Ernie's machine that spewed up that green goo.

It was the house.

And as that frightening thought lingered in Kody's mind, she glanced up and saw a wisp of light at the window.

The light shimmered into a pale white mist. And inside the mist, Kody recognized her sister.

"Cally!"

As she called out the name, the light faded. The image vanished.

Kody blinked.

"Kody—are you okay?" Bo demanded, hands pressed against the waist of his baggy chinos.

"Uh—yeah. I guess," Kody replied uncertainly. Her eyes on the window. She expected to see Cally appear once more. She *wanted* to see Cally appear.

"We're lighting the dining room for tomorrow morning," Bo told them. "We'll shoot the attic scene later." He checked through some pages on the clipboard. Then he gazed at the middle-aged actor sitting beside Persia on the couch. "This will be your first scene, Burt," he said.

Kody turned her attention to Burt Martindale, the actor chosen to play her father. He had just been cast and arrived on the set late. Kody had said hello to him. Nothing more.

He seemed friendly. He had twinkling blue eyes under his thinning blond hair and a warm smile. It bothered Kody that Burt didn't look at all like her real father. But, she told herself, this *was* the movies.

"I hope I have an easier time of it than you!" Burt called across the room to Kody.

"I hope so," Kody replied, sighing.

"Do you know how to swim?" Persia asked Burt dryly.

"Not funny, Persia," Bo said sternly. "No jokes. I mean it." He glanced nervously around the room. "Marge and Noah—where are you?"

Marge Andersen raised her hand above her head and waved at Bo. She was a frail-looking actress with short blond hair and a fretful expression, chosen to play Kody's mother.

Marge was very shy and quiet, Kody had discovered during their rehearsals in Los Angeles. She sat near the window beside Noah Klein, the ten-year-old who played Kody's brother James.

"I want to block out the dinner scene with the actors," Bo announced. "The rest of you have your assignments. We're going to shoot this first thing tomorrow. And," he added, saying each word slowly and distinctly, *"there will be no slipups or problems.* Understood?"

Murmured agreements and comments filled the air as everyone stood up and moved quickly from the living room.

Kody didn't feel at all like reading through the dining room scene. She was eager to find Cally.

Cally had appeared to her by the window. Cally

must want to talk to me, Kody told herself. If only I could go find her.

But Kody knew she had no choice. She had to rehearse the frightening scene.

Pulling herself up, she started to follow Bo and the others into the dining room. But Persia stepped in front of her, blocking Kody's path.

"Kody, does your hair look a little green from that awful gunk, or is it just the lighting in here?" Persia asked, a cruel smile on her full, dark lips.

"Persia, I'm really in no mood—" Kody started to say.

"Yes, you *look* really tired," Persia commented. "I just wanted to get your approval of an idea I told to Bo."

"An idea?" Kody asked warily.

"Well, just a seating idea," Persia replied. "I know we were supposed to be across from each other at the table when Burt stabs himself. But I thought it would be more tense if we sat side by side, and if maybe you and I had some sort of argument about the carving knife."

"Huh?" Kody's face twisted in confusion.

"You know. To show how competitive we two sisters are," Persia continued. "Bo loved the idea. Really."

"Well, okay—" Kody started to agree.

"I put myself on your left because that's my better side," Persia told her. "Is that okay, Kody? I wasn't sure *which* is your better side!"

What a cruel dig, Kody thought bitterly. Persia really is the meanest person I ever met.

Without replying, she stepped past Persia and made her way into the dining room. The room was cluttered with equipment. Workers on the lighting and sound crew scrambled over every inch, preparing for the next morning's shoot.

Two young women, the prop master and her assistant, were busily setting the table. Kody eased around a boom mike, then started toward Bo and the others at the head of the table.

But the object lying in the center of the white linen tablecloth made her stop—and stare.

A large black-handled carving knife. The fat blade gleamed under the harsh overhead lights.

Kody's vision blurred. And in the shimmery glow of the knife blade, she saw her real family. Cally and James and her mother and father, sitting around a similar table in this same dining room, two years ago.

Such a happy scene.

Their first dinner in this, their new house.

Mr. Frasier stood to carve the roast beef. Cally got up from her chair and headed for the kitchen. As Cally passed behind him, the knife flew up as if pushed by an unseen hand.

The family watched in shock as the knife plunged deep into Mr. Frasier's side.

The happy dinner ended in cries and panic.

The horror had begun.

"I'm going to put you at the head of the table, Burt," Kody heard Bo saying in the back of her mind.

"And, Marge, let's try to get you within reach of him here on the side."

"What about me? I thought I sat closest to the father," Kody heard Noah say.

Bo's reply faded into the background as Kody found herself staring at the gleaming carving knife.

This knife is just a prop.

No one is really going to get stabbed this time, Kody told herself.

So why do I have such a bad feeling, such a cold, cold feeling about this knife?

Chapter 23

Kody hid in her trailer, waiting for everyone to leave for the day.

She spent some time going over the revised pages of the script for the dining room scene. Persia's idea is really silly, Kody thought. Cally and I weren't like that. I can't imagine two teenage girls who are so competitive that they argue over who gets to pass a knife to their father.

I can't believe that Bo likes the idea, Kody thought, staring out the trailer window as the sun lowered behind the trees. He says it's good character development.

Well—fine.

Of course I'll play the scene without making a fuss. I

mean, no one asked my opinion anyway. Persia is the pro, after all.

And what am I? Kody thought unhappily.

I'm the freak. I'm the real-life freak people can point to in the movie theater and say to each other, "Did you know she's the real sister?"

Kody let out a bitter sigh.

I want to *see* my real sister, she thought.

Cally is in the house. I saw her. And tonight I'm going to find her.

Or maybe she'll find me.

Kody tried to phone Rob at the hospital. But the cellular phone in the trailer didn't seem to be working. She heard a busy signal as soon as she clicked it on.

Settling onto the couch to wait for the house to empty out, she soon drifted into an uneasy sleep. She dreamed of her parents. She was home with them in Los Angeles. They were all eating doughnuts. Big, sugary doughnuts.

But the sickening, putrid taste of the green goo invaded Kody's dream. The doughnuts smelled so rotten, like decayed, maggoty meat. And they tasted even worse.

Kody woke up gagging.

She sat up, swallowing hard, shaking her head to chase away the ugly dream.

The sky was dark, she saw. She must have slept for an hour or two. She peered out the trailer window at the house. Also dark.

"Cally, I'm going to find you tonight," she murmured out loud.

She bent over the mirror and pushed back her blond hair with both hands. Then she quickly rubbed on some clear lip gloss. Her heart pounding, she stepped down from the trailer, closing the door softly behind her.

A warm breeze made the tall grass rustle as Kody made her way over the lawn to the house. Crickets started a shrill symphony as she reached the front porch.

I feel so nervous, Kody realized.

The nap hadn't helped to calm her. It had somehow made her even edgier.

The front door creaked loudly as she pushed it open.

The old haunted-house special effect, she thought.

She stepped into the front entryway. A rectangle of light from the living room slid over the carpet. Someone must have left a lamp on.

Kody stepped into the light and gazed into the living room. Dark metal equipment boxes were stacked in front of the fireplace. Several microphones rested near coils of electrical cable against the far wall.

Kody turned back into the hallway. Where shall I look first? she asked herself, wishing her heart would stop racing, wishing her hands didn't feel so cold and wet.

She took a step toward the kitchen.

Then she heard the voice, soft as a whisper: *"Kody, here I am."*

"Oh!" Kody uttered a shocked cry and spun around.

"Are you looking for me?" Cally's voice. Soft and playful.

"Y-yes," Kody stammered. "I—want to see you, Cally. I miss you."

"Follow me, Kody." Cally's voice moved toward the back hall.

"I can't believe it's really you!" Kody cried, feeling her emotions swell. She didn't know how much longer she could hold back the tears. "Where are you, Cally? Can I see you? Can I *hug* you?"

"Follow me," Cally repeated. *"I'm right here, Kody."*

In the dim hall light, Kody saw that the door to the basement stood open. Cally's voice seemed to come from the doorway.

Kody realized her entire body was trembling with excitement. "Do you want me to come downstairs, Cally? Can't we talk up here? Can't I see you now?"

"Soon," Cally replied, her voice soft and cool. *"Come downstairs with me, Kody. Don't be afraid."*

Kody hesitated at the top of the basement stairs.

What about the rats? What about the explosives?

"Don't be afraid," Cally instructed. *"Come down with me, Kody. I've waited so long to talk to you."*

"Me too!" Kody cried. Forgetting her fear, she plunged down the stairs.

She stopped at the bottom and waited for her eyes to adjust to the darkness. "Where are you, Cally? It's so dark down here."

"This way, Kody. I want to show you a special place."

Kody fumbled against the wall, found the switch, clicked on the basement light. The crates of explosives, piled in the center of the floor, came into view. Kody saw a long wire stretching from the crates, leading to a box with a slender plunger—the detonator.

That's weird, she thought. Has Bo wired the explosives for the end of the movie even though we haven't even begun shooting?

"Kody—please hurry. I'm so eager to talk to you." Cally's voice made Kody turn away from the wooden crates.

"Where are you?" Kody called. "Let me see you—please!"

"I'm over here. Can't you hurry?" Cally's voice floated to Kody from across the basement.

Making her way past the explosives, Kody spotted a narrow doorway against the far wall. "I never knew there was another room down here," she told her sister.

She heard a scuttling sound behind her. The scratch of a rat's claws. The sound sent a chill down her back.

Kody hurried through the narrow doorway, and found herself in a dimly lit room no bigger than a closet. A bare light bulb hung from a frayed cord, casting a harsh yellow glow over the stone walls and concrete floor. A low three-legged stool stood against the back wall, the only furniture.

"Cally? Are you in here?" Kody whispered.

"Yes. Here I am."

A wisp of pale white light flickered above the stool.

The light shimmered and grew until it resembled a small cloud.

Kody let out a happy cry as Cally stepped out from the cloud.

"I *knew* I'd see you again!" Kody exclaimed, her voice breaking with emotion.

A smile spread across Cally's face. Her green eyes sparkled like bright emeralds. Her pale skin appeared to shimmer.

Tears rolled down Kody's cheeks. She spread her arms, dove forward, and wrapped her sister in a hug.

"Oh." Kody pulled back, unable to hide her surprise. "Cally—you're so *cold!*"

Cally's smile grew wider. Her eyes glowed so brightly, Kody had to lower her gaze.

"I've waited so long for this, Kody," the ghost said, ignoring Kody's surprised cry.

Kody felt the cold mist sweep over her.

Cally seemed to fade behind the cloud.

The mist billowed, folding Kody inside.

Cally became a shadow in the mist. The shadow loomed over Kody.

The billowing cold made Kody shudder. The shadow rolled down over her like darkness falling.

"Cally—no!" Kody managed to cry out. "Cally—what are you *doing* to me?"

Chapter 24

"Over here, Kody," Bo said, gesturing with his clipboard to the chair at the dining room table beside Persia. "Have you been to Makeup?"

"Can't you tell?" Kody teased.

Everyone seemed to be in a better mood. Maybe they could actually get a scene on film.

The night before, Bo had spent an hour on the phone with the studio execs. He'd told them things were going well, except for a few minor accidents.

What a lie! So far, all he'd managed to get on film were some outside shots of the house. Now he had to knuckle down and get to work.

He guided Kody to her place at the dining room table beside Persia. Then he discussed a lighting problem with one of the crew. He greeted Burt and Marge and asked Noah to get rid of his gum. One of the assistants hurried over to take the gum from the boy.

Bo turned back to the actors. Kody sat rigidly beside Persia, who stared at her dark nails and didn't even bother to look up or say good morning.

"Nice day," Kody said, scooting her chair in.

Persia muttered something under her breath in reply.

"How is everyone today?" Bo called cheerily, resting his hands on Burt's shoulders. "I love having a big roast beef dinner at seven in the morning, don't you?"

Burt and Marge laughed. Noah yawned and slid down in his chair so that his head barely poked over the table.

"Bo, I can't believe we're actually going to shoot a scene," Persia remarked, rolling her eyes. She turned to Kody. "Is my wig on straight? Yours is a little crooked."

"I'm not wearing a wig," Kody replied sharply.

"That's your real hair?" Persia asked, pretending to be surprised. "I told my hairdresser not to make the wig so neat. I mean, your hair is always so—free. Since I'm stuck playing you, I wanted my hair to have that same disheveled look."

"Thanks," Kody replied sarcastically.

"Persia, give her a break," Bo interrupted. He stepped back toward the camera. "One run-through. Then we shoot." He turned toward the back and shouted, "Props! Let's get the food out, okay?"

"Coming right out. We're spraying the meat!" a woman's voice called from the kitchen.

"That's to make it shine and look yummy," Bo explained to Kody. He turned to Persia. "While we're waiting, let's block out your knife-fight idea. I'm still not sure I get it."

"It's just a little competitive moment between the sisters," Persia told him impatiently. "Kody always feels second best, right? She always feels left out. Cally is the beauty and the one with all the brains and all the luck and blah blah blah."

"We know all that," Bo said, glancing at his watch.

"So when Dad says 'Pass the carving knife,' both sisters grab for it at the same time," Persia continued. "And neither one wants to let go. They have a short tug-of-war, that's all. Just to show how competitive Kody feels."

"Let me see how it'll work," Bo said, rubbing the dark stubble on his chin. "Run through it for me once."

Burt passed the black-handled carving knife over to Persia.

Persia placed it in front of her. "Now, be careful and don't cut yourself," she told Kody as if talking to a three-year-old.

"You should move the knife more between us," Kody suggested. "That would make it more logical for me to reach for it."

Persia slid the knife closer to Kody. "Perhaps you could give Kody a little direction," Persia suggested to Bo. "I know that Kody hasn't had any improv training. I don't want to get her any more tense than she already is. The poor thing is quivering like jelly."

"I *am not!*" Kody protested shrilly, her face bright red.

"Let's just play through the scene, okay?" Bo told Persia. "I'm not so sure it's going to work anyway."

"It'll work if she can handle it," Persia replied coolly.

"Burt—give them some kind of cue," Bo instructed.

"Then, when the two sisters struggle over the knife, should I try to stop it?" Marge asked.

"Let's see how it plays," Bo replied, stepping back. "Let's go. Action."

Burt cleared his throat. "This roast beef looks delicious," he said, smiling down at an empty platter. "Would you please pass the carving knife?"

Persia reached for the knife.

But Kody grabbed it first.

She lifted it by the handle, raised it straight up, then brought the blade down hard, plunging it through the back of Persia's hand, pinning Persia's hand to the table.

Chapter 25

Bo stared frozen in shock as Kody let go of the knife and calmly lowered her hands to her lap.

Persia didn't start screaming until the bright red blood began to pour over the back of her hand.

It took a second for everyone to realize what had happened. Someone had replaced the prop knife with a real one!

Frantically, she tried to tug her hand up from the table—which made the blade cut deeper.

Blood flowed over her hand, puddled beneath it.

"You *idiot!* You *idiot!*" she shrieked at Kody.

"It's not my fault," Kody cried, jumping to her feet. "Someone switched the knives. It was supposed to be a prop knife!"

They all watched Kody step back, her hands pressed against her cheeks as everyone crowded to the table to help Persia. The room filled with startled cries and shouts of alarm.

"Call a doctor! Just call a doctor!" Bo shouted. He tossed his clipboard furiously against the wall.

"What is going on here?" Bo asked, trying to force down his anger and frustration.

Two crew members struggled to pull the knife from the table to free Persia's hand. Persia screamed and cried, her eyes shut, her face twisted in agony. "I'm going to bleed to death! Somebody—do something!"

"Did someone call a doctor?" Bo cried. Everyone was screaming, shouting out instructions, shouting their disbelief. The racket was deafening. And over the roar came Persia's shrill, angry wails.

A few seconds later they heard Persia's high-pitched squeal when the knife was finally pulled out of her hand. They stared at the widening bloodstain on the white tablecloth. Two men were wrapping a white linen napkin around Persia's hand. The blood soaked quickly through the napkin.

"Is a doctor on the way?"

"Did you call 911?"

"Is that an ambulance outside?"

Confused and frightened shouts filled the house.

As two paramedics burst into the room, Bo saw Kody backing away. He moved quickly to confront her. "I need to speak to you."

She hesitated, squinting against the bright white lights.

"I need to speak to you now," Bo insisted, hands pressed tensely against his waist.

"Wh-what is it?" Kody stammered.

"I've tried to be understanding," Bo said, sighing at Kody. "But this time it's gone too far. I can't let this go on. Too many people have gotten hurt."

"I feel so terrible," Kody said.

Bo frowned at her. "Too many incidents. Too many accidents," he murmured.

She swallowed hard. "I don't understand."

"I'm not superstitious," Bo told her. He had to raise his voice to be heard over Persia's cries from the table. "But it's pretty obvious to me that this picture is jinxed."

Kody's mouth dropped. "I still don't understand."

"I don't either," Bo replied. "But it must have something to do with you, Kody. Something to do with the fact that you lived in this house, that you experienced its evil."

"But, Bo—" Kody started to say, shielding her eyes from the bright spotlight.

He raised a hand to silence her. "So much has gone wrong since we arrived here," he said, sighing. "And each time, you have been there, Kody. Each time, you were standing there while something horrible happened. I'm not saying you're the cause of our problems. I'm not saying you're responsible. But you're the jinx. I know you are."

"Bo—that's crazy!" Kody cried. "You don't really believe that I—"

Bo nodded solemnly. "I have to ask you to leave,"

he said softly. "I have to remove you from the picture."

He expected her to lower her eyes and retreat quickly. He expected tears. He expected her to plead and beg for another chance.

Instead, Kody startled him by reacting angrily. "No, you don't," she replied sharply. "No way, Bo. No way I'm leaving."

"I'm really sorry—" Bo said.

"No. *I'm* the one who is sorry!" Kody declared.

She lifted the big, glowing spotlight by its pole, swung it hard—and slammed the front of the light into Bo's face.

Stunned as the pain burst over him, he tossed up his arms and staggered back.

But she kept the light pressed against his face until his skin sizzled.

When she finally tossed the light to the floor, the side of Bo's face smoked. He let out a weak gurgling sound and slumped to the floor.

Before he lost consciousness, he heard Kody's cheerful shout to the others: "Okay, everybody! That's a wrap!"

Chapter 26

Kody hunched down on the low stool, struggling against the ropes that held her arms and legs. The handkerchief tied around her face as a gag choked her dry throat.

She had twisted and pulled at the ropes for hours. With no success.

How long had she been locked down in the basement?

Terrified and exhausted, she had lost track of the time. She knew it must be daytime. She heard the voices above her head, heard the screams, heard all the commotion.

She knew Cally had taken her place. She knew Cally was upstairs in the dining room, pretending to be her.

And now Kody knew that Cally had become evil.

Cally was not Cally anymore.

The night before, the shadow of Cally had swept over Kody, darkened over her, darkened until Kody felt as if she were floating in a cold, bottomless cavern.

In the icy darkness Kody felt Cally's evil. She felt Cally's anger, felt the hatred that filled her heart.

When the darkness lifted, Kody found herself locked in the bare basement room. Gagged. Her ankles tied together. Her hands tied behind her back.

Cally, she realized, had lured her there and then imprisoned her, determined to take her place.

And now what was Cally doing upstairs?

As Kody sat hunched over on the low stool, struggling to hear, other sounds invaded her ears.

The scratching, scuttling sounds. The swish of tails being dragged over the basement floor.

The rats. So close. So close Kody thought she could hear them breathe.

She heard a shrill hiss.

The scratching grew nearer.

Kody struggled awkwardly to her feet and glanced around the walls of the small room.

Where were the rats? Why did they sound so close?

Her heart began to thud in her chest. She swallowed hard.

Another hiss, almost like dry laughter.

The scratch of sharp rat claws.

Where? Where are they?

Kody spun to the door. Then turned back.

And spotted the hole in the wall. A slender crack down near the floor.

Just a crack. But big enough for a rat to crawl through.

Or several rats.

Staring hard at the crack between two stones, she dropped to her knees. She lowered her head to the crack—and listened.

Scratching. A shrill screeching hiss.

Yes. The rats were on the other side, Kody realized.

But could they squeeze through the crack?

Were they going to?

Chapter 27

Kody shuddered as she lowered her face to the crack and peered through it. To her surprise, she saw light on the other side.

Tilting her head down to see, the gag popped off Kody's face. She swallowed hard.

As her eyes focused, she saw a rat sitting on its haunches.

Another rat, its scraggly whiskers twitching, bared its teeth and hissed at the first rat.

Kody's breath caught in her throat as she struggled to see the other room clearly. How many rats were in that room?

"There, there, dear."

The sound of the woman's voice made Kody jerk

back. Startled, she raised herself on her knees and struggled to catch her breath.

"There, there. That's a dear." The voice sounded so familiar.

But who would be down in the basement? And whom was the woman talking to?

Struggling to balance, Kody took a deep breath and lowered her face once again to the slender crack in the wall.

The rats had moved, she saw. Or perhaps these were different rats. One of them, a plump brown creature with a long, hairy tail, scuttled in quick circles.

"Stop that, dear. You'll only tire yourself," the woman's voice scolded.

Kody raised her eyes and discovered the owner of the voice.

Mrs. Nordstrom!

The housekeeper sat on a low stool similar to the one in Kody's small room, bending and talking to the rats at her feet.

No! Kody thought. *This is a dream! This can't be real!*

Shifting her body to get a better view, Kody squinted hard into the next room—and saw two other familiar figures seated beside Mrs. Nordstrom.

"Look at him run circles!" Mr. Hankers exclaimed, elbowing Mr. Lurie in the ribs.

"Don't tire yourself," Mrs. Nordstrom scolded the circling rat.

Mr. Hankers tore off a strip of cheese from a slice he held between both hands and tossed it to the rat. The other rats—at least six or seven of them—began to screech excitedly and jump up and down on Mr. Hankers's pants legs.

Mr. Hankers was supposed to *kill* the rats! Kody told herself, staring in shock. Instead, he's feeding them!

Feeling her throat tighten in disgust, Kody watched Mr. Lurie, the real estate agent, reach down and pick up a fat gray rat in his fist. The rat squawked and thrashed. Laughing, Mr. Lurie set the creature down on the shoulder of his gray suit jacket.

The rat immediately leaped to the floor.

"Haw-haw!" Mrs. Nordstrom cackled. "He doesn't like you!"

"Aw, they don't like you either," Mr. Lurie griped sourly.

Mrs. Nordstrom flashed him a wink. "Oh, yeah? Watch this."

As Kody watched with growing revulsion, Mrs. Nordstrom lowered both hands to the floor. "Come on, fellas," she cooed.

A rat scuttled onto each hand. A pleased grin spread over Mrs. Nordstrom's face. She raised them up, holding the rats in her palms. Then she started to giggle as the rats stretched out their claws and nibbled and gnawed on her fingers.

"Oh! How gross!"

Kody didn't realize she had cried out.

She saw Mrs. Nordstrom glance up from the gnawing rats.

Kody gasped.

Did she hear me?

What is she going to do?

Chapter 28

"Come on, dear. Leave me a little skin on that finger," Mrs. Nordstrom scolded one of the rats.

"He likes to suck the blood," Mr. Hankers said, snickering.

Kody sighed with relief. They hadn't heard her. She dropped back onto the stool, her head spinning with questions.

Why were these three people sitting in the hidden basement room? Did they live there?

Why were they playing with the rats, talking to them, letting the ugly creatures chew their fingers?

Why? Why? Why?

The questions spun around and around in Kody's mind as if caught in a whirling cyclone.

I've got to get out of here, she told herself. I've got to get away!

She struggled again to loosen the ropes—but a word spoken by Mrs. Nordstrom on the other side of the wall made Kody stop. The word was *Cally.*

What is she saying about my sister? Kody wondered. She lowered her face to the crack in the wall and struggled to hear.

"Cally is a good girl," Mrs. Nordstrom was saying, tenderly stroking the scraggly gray fur on the back of the rat in her hand.

"She *was* a good girl," Mr. Lurie commented. "But then we got hold of her."

All three of them laughed.

"I said she's good because she does everything we tell her," Mrs. Nordstrom said. She sighed and set the rat down on the floor. It scrabbled over to join the others.

"You like them obedient, don't you!" Mr. Hankers said, chuckling.

"Obedient and ignorant," Mrs. Nordstrom replied, tossing the rats a slice of cheese and watching them battle over it. "That girl thinks she's obeying her own will."

All three of them laughed as if Mrs. Nordstrom had cracked a very funny joke.

Kody pulled back from the wall. She shut her eyes, trying to figure out what she had just heard.

They just explained why Cally is so evil, she realized. I was right when I thought that Cally isn't Cally.

Those three weird people are controlling her.

They've tricked Cally into obeying their wishes. Or maybe they've possessed her somehow.

Kody realized she didn't understand any of it. She knew only that she was now afraid for Cally as well as for herself.

Shutting her eyes, she tried to think clearly. But nothing made any sense.

She lost track of time again.

The house had become silent. The excited, shouting voices from upstairs had all vanished. No footsteps. No sounds at all.

What am I going to do? Kody asked herself.

What *can* I do?

When she opened her eyes, Cally was standing in front of her.

Kody gasped and jumped to her feet. "Cally—!"

Cally's green eyes stared coldly at her. Her expression revealed no emotion at all.

"Cally—what happened upstairs? What is going on?"

Her sister's ghost didn't reply. Instead, she moved menacingly toward Kody.

"No!" Kody shrieked, feeling terror in her chest. "Cally—no! What are you going to do?"

"Goodbye, sister," Cally replied coldly. *"Goodbye forever."*

Chapter 29

"No. Cally—please!" Kody begged as the ghost floated nearer. "Don't hurt me!"

Cally's pale lips twisted in an amused smile. "Hurt you? I don't need to." She pulled the ropes off Kody's arms and legs. Then she waved to the open doorway. "Go."

Kody's entire body trembled as she stared at her sister's cruel smile.

"Go," Cally repeated. "The door is open, Kody." And then she shouted impatiently, *"Go!"*

"But—" Kody started to the door, then hesitated. "You're not going to kill me?" she choked out.

"No need," Cally replied casually. "I've already taken care of you, Kody."

"Wh-what do you mean?" Kody stammered, edging toward the door.

"You did some bad things upstairs this morning," Cally replied, her green eyes glowing. "You stabbed Persia Bryce. And then you held a spotlight to the director's face. You burned him so badly, his own mother won't recognize him!"

"No!" Kody cried in horror. "Cally, you didn't—!"

Cally nodded, her smile growing wider. "I did. I'm sorry, Kody. I don't think you're going to be a movie star after all. I think you're going to spend a lot of years in prison—or in a mental hospital."

Kody struggled to speak. Had Cally really ruined her life?

Why? Why did Cally hate her so much?

It is the evil in the house, Kody told herself. It's the three evil people in the next room. They're controlling Cally. They're *making* Cally do these things.

Kody took a deep breath. I came here to keep a promise, she remembered. I came back here to help Cally. And I have to try to do that.

"Go!" Cally shouted angrily, pointing to the door. "Hurry. Get out of here." And then she added bitterly, "Have a nice life."

Kody took a step toward her sister. "I won't go until you listen to me," she insisted.

Cally's mouth twisted into a sneer. "You have nothing to say to me."

"Yes, I do," Kody replied, gathering her courage. "Do you remember the story your boyfriend Anthony told us about this house? Do you remember? He said that when the workers dug the foundation, they found bodies buried in the ground? The people buried here were the victims of Angelica and Simon Fear. Remember?"

"So what?" Cally snapped.

"The house was built on top of their graves," Kody continued, her voice trembling. "It's an evil place, Cally. Filled with evil. And somehow—the three people in the next room—Mrs. Nordstrom and the two men—they're controlling you. They're evil too and they—"

"Who?" Cally screamed, her eyes flashing angrily. The dust sparkled up around her as she swirled closer. "What are you *talking* about?"

"In the next room," Kody told her, pointing to the wall. "They play with the rats. They were supposed to be working for us. But, instead, they—they—" Kody stopped. She could see from Cally's bewildered expression that she had no idea what power these three people had over her.

"Have a nice time at the mental hospital," Cally said softly. She let out a bitter laugh. "Send me a postcard."

"No!" Kody cried, grabbing her sister's hand. It felt so cold, Kody nearly dropped it. But she managed to hold on, and tugged her sister to the small hole in the wall.

"I'm not crazy," Kody insisted. "Take a look through there, Cally. I'm not crazy. I want you to see the truth. I know this isn't you. I know you're not cruel and evil. It's *them,* Cally. It's them. Take a look. Please!"

Cally made no move toward the narrow hole. "I really don't care," she said flatly, her voice as dry as air. "I'm dead. I don't care about holes in the wall."

"Please!" Kody begged. "Take a look at them. Take a look at their evil faces. They're controlling you. They're using you. I heard them talk about it. I heard them laugh about it. They're making you do these horrible things."

Cally hesitated, then floated down and peered through the crack in the wall.

Kody stood tensely in the center of the small room, watching her sister. Cally seemed to freeze there. She didn't move or blink. She stared into the other room for several minutes, her face completely expressionless.

When she rose up and turned back to Kody, her expression had softened. The angry glow had faded from her eyes.

"Did you see them?" Kody asked eagerly. "Did you see them with the rats?"

Cally didn't reply. She floated away from the wall, her pale face shimmering in and out of focus, her expression thoughtful.

"Did you see them?" Kody insisted. "Do you believe me now?"

Cally stared at Kody as if gazing right through her. "Come with me, Kody," she whispered finally. "I will get you out of this house."

Kody let out a sigh of relief. Cally *believes* me! she

told herself. I *knew* I could reach her. I *knew* I could show her the truth.

But how can I help her? How?

"The explosives!" Kody cried. "We can blow up the house, blow up all the evil."

Cally raised a finger to her lips to silence Kody. "Never mind that," she said softly. "Let me get you out of here. Come with me. Hurry."

Cally swept past Kody and led the way to the door. Her heart pounding, Kody followed close behind.

Out into the basement. Gray evening light floated in from the narrow window, casting long shadows across the floor.

"Thank you, Cally," a voice said.

Kody let out a low cry as Mrs. Nordstrom stepped forward, followed by Mr. Hankers and Mr. Lurie.

"Thank you for bringing her to us, Cally," Mrs. Nordstrom said, smiling warmly. "Now we will make sure you get your revenge."

Chapter 30

"You *tricked* me!" Kody screeched at her sister. "You *betrayed* me!"

Mrs. Nordstrom and the two men moved nearer, circling Kody, their faces set, their eyes narrowed, cold and menacing.

"Cally—I'm your sister! Your twin! How *could* you?" Kody shrieked, so frightened she didn't recognize her own voice.

Cally's face remained blank and uncaring. "I wouldn't betray you," she replied softly. "You showed me the truth. Run to the stairs, Kody. Run now! I will protect you from them."

Kody gasped as Mrs. Nordstrom and the two men moved closer. Was this just a trick? Or was Cally really going to protect her, to save her?

"Run!" Cally screamed.

Kody began backing toward the stairs, her eyes on the three people.

"Hurry! Run!" Cally urged.

But Kody stopped and stared in horror as Mrs. Nordstrom and the two men began to change.

Their skin bubbled and blistered, darkening to a splotchy gray. Short, stubbly hair sprouted all over their faces and hands.

Slowly, their faces stretched. Their noses lengthened into dark, hairy snouts. Sticky white whiskers twitched over jagged yellow teeth. Snakelike red tongues flicked over the gnarled teeth. Their wet eyes shriveled behind the twitching snouts to black marbles.

Kody gaped in shock as the three figures shrank and their clothing fell away.

Out from under the clothing darted three plump gray rats.

Scuttling out from her skirt, Mrs. Nordstrom hissed at Kody and raised her rat claws menacingly.

Mr. Lurie snapped his long, pink tail behind him. A line of drool fell from Mr. Hankers's snarling mouth as he scratched the gray fur of his belly with both claws.

"No!" Kody cried in a trembling, weak voice. "No! You—you can't be—!"

She backed to the stairs, her eyes wide in terror and disbelief.

Rats. They're rats. All three of them.

Mrs. Nordstrom bared her teeth and, with a shrill hiss, leaped at Kody's ankle.

Kody cried out and kicked the plump rat hard. Her sneaker made a soft *plop* as it collided with the hissing rat, sending it sprawling on its back beside its two snarling companions.

"Run, Kody! Run!" Cally was screaming.

And as she backed toward the stairs, Kody saw more rats slithering out into the basement.

From behind the furnace, from behind the crates of explosives, from holes in the walls and cracks in the floor, the rats—dozens and dozens of them—crept out.

Screeching and hissing, sweeping their hairless pink tails behind them, rats blanketed the floor, a sea of gnarled teeth and glowing eyes.

Struggling to move her trembling legs, Kody grabbed the railing and pulled herself onto the first step.

"Hurry!" Cally urged, moving toward the explosives detonator. "Kody—hurry!"

The floor appeared to seethe and toss. So many gray bodies rushing forward, screeching and hissing and snapping their jaws.

"But wh-what about you?" Kody stammered.

"I'm dead!" came Cally's heartbreaking reply.

The screeching of the rats drowned out Kody's sob.

The rats suddenly swept forward, hissing and whistling. Their claws thrashed the air as they scuttled to the stairs.

"Ow!" Kody shrieked as a rat scratched its claw against her leg. A thousand eyes glared hungrily, moving toward her.

Taking one last look at her sister, she turned and forced her legs to carry her up the stairs.

Into the hallway, the screeching, the hissing, the sound of scrabbling feet following her, driving her forward, making her run.

Past the dark living room. Out the front door.

Into the darkness of the front yard.

Running across the grass. Gasping for air. The horrifying sounds of the rats lingering in her ears.

Kody was halfway to the street when the force of the explosion threw her to the ground.

"Ohhhhh." Landing hard on her knees and elbows, she let out a groan.

The ground shook. She turned back to the house in time to see the blinding white burst.

As bright as the sun.

I can't see! Kody thought.

And then the white darkened to scarlet.

A roar louder than thunder made her cover her ears.

The roof shot up, shattering as it flew, rising above the dark trees. And then a wall of flame rose over the house. A roaring tidal wave of fire.

"Noooooooo!"

Kody couldn't hear her own terrified wail over the crackling thunder of the blaze.

Squinting into the fiery red brightness, she began to see dark shapes. Rat bodies, thrashing wildly, flying helplessly in the raging flames. Hundreds of rats, shooting skyward in the fire, sizzling, burning as they flew.

Kody felt her stomach heave, felt the disgust rise up in her. But she couldn't take her eyes away from the fiery sky, from the charred black rat bodies that flew over the roaring flames.

And then human forms twisted up in the fire. Black shadows. The dark, tortured spirits of those buried under the house. Men and women, wailing and howling, thrashing in the flames as they rose higher, higher, and disappeared into the starless black sky.

Kody cried out as a wall crashed to the ground. Red embers shot out in all directions.

Gripped with horror, she stared. Stared as the mournful howls faded into the roar of the flames. Stared as the tortured bodies twisted up into the smoke-blackened sky.

Stared as the wall of flames swallowed the house, consuming the evil, burning it all away.

On her knees on the cool, soft grass, Kody stared into the flames, letting the heat of the fire dry her tears.

"I'm sorry, Cally," she murmured softly. "I'm so sorry. I'm so sorry. . . .

"I'm sorry I didn't get a chance to say goodbye."

Chapter 31

"What's up with you? Don't you ever want to go out?" Rob asked.

Kody crossed the room and sat down across from him on the small, matching white leather armchair. "The police called again this morning. It's been weeks since the explosion, and they still can't figure out what happened. Everyone had a different story, and one version is stranger than the next. And they still have trouble believing that it was Cally, not me, who did all those horrible things."

Kody sighed. "Fortunately, they're going to drop it. Of course, I'll still have to go for therapy twice a week. But I'm glad no one is pressing charges."

"Yeah," agreed Rob. "I just want to forget the whole thing."

"Me too. Anyway, I just feel like staying in. My parents are out for the night. I ordered a pizza."

Rob made a face. "Pizza again?"

"I like pizza," Kody insisted. "What can I say? I have simple tastes."

"You *must* have simple tastes. You're going out with *me!*" Rob joked.

It was three weeks after the fire that had destroyed 99 Fear Street—and put an end to the movie production.

Back in her parents' apartment in Los Angeles, Kody remained dazed by all that had happened. But Rob had been coming over nearly every day. He had managed to get her to smile and laugh again and feel almost normal.

"I auditioned for a commercial this afternoon," he told her.

"That's great!" Kody replied enthusiastically.

"It's for another dog food. But this time I don't have to bark," Rob told her.

They both laughed.

The doorbell rang.

"That's the pizza," Kody told him, climbing to her feet. "Get the door. I'll go get some Cokes."

Kody hurried to the kitchen and pulled two cans of Coke from the refrigerator. When she returned to the living room, she was surprised to see Rob holding a large brown envelope.

"Not the pizza," he said. He removed a videocassette from the envelope. A note was taped to the box. Kody pulled it off and read it:

> Here's a collector's item for you, Kody. It's the only film that was shot at 99 Fear Street. Talk about a big finish!
>
> Better luck to us all!
> Sam McCarthy

"Who's McCarthy?" Rob asked, leaning over her shoulder to read the note.

"You remember," Kody said softly. "He was the associate producer. You know. His hand—it was mangled in the garbage disposal."

Rob nodded, then slowly pulled the tape from the box. "Do you want to see it? Maybe we shouldn't. It might upset you."

Kody stared at the tape thoughtfully. "Put it on," she instructed him. "If it starts to get upsetting, we'll turn it off."

Rob crossed the room to the video player. He clicked on the TV, then pushed the cassette into the VCR. Then he sat down beside Kody on the couch to watch.

The screen was gray for a while. There was no sound.

Then the screen suddenly blazed with color. Bright flashes of red and yellow.

"It—it's the fire!" Kody exclaimed, leaning closer to the screen. "I don't believe it, Rob! Somebody filmed the fire! They must have been shooting exterior shots for the end!"

"Look—there goes a wall!" Rob cried.

The red glare of the TV screen reflected off their faces as they leaned forward to see better.

The camera slid closer. The screen seemed to glow with bright white light.

"Oh!" Kody let out a low cry as the faded image of a girl appeared inside the light, her features too faint to recognize.

"Who *is* that?" Rob cried. "Was someone caught in the fire?"

Kody rested her hand on his, but didn't reply. Her entire body tensed as she leaned toward the screen.

The girl in the fire raised one hand and waved it. A long, slow, sad wave.

"I don't get it. What *is* that?" Rob asked impatiently.

Kody squeezed his hand. She let the tears roll down her cheeks.

"That's my sister saying goodbye."

About the Author

"Where do you get your ideas?"

That's the question that R. L. Stine is asked most often. "I don't know where my ideas come from," he says. "But I do know that I have a lot more scary stories in my mind that I can't wait to write."

So far, he has written more than fifty mysteries and thrillers for young people, all of them bestsellers.

Bob grew up in Columbus, Ohio. Today he lives in an apartment near Central Park in New York City with his wife, Jane, and fourteen-year-old son, Matt.

THE NIGHTMARES NEVER END . . . WHEN YOU VISIT

Next . . .

THE MIND READER

(Coming in November 1994)

All her life Ellie Anderson has had visions. When she was young, she always knew what her grandmother was cooking for dinner or when her grandfather was going into town—even before they did.

Then Ellie finds the body of a young girl in the woods, and her visions become terrifying. Tormented by violent images, Ellie struggles to make sense of them. Could they be a warning about the new boy in her life? Or are they a desperate cry for help from beyond the grave?